JUST THE WAY YOU ARE

"What are you asking me, Dee?" her mother said. "It sounds as if you want to be more serious—more like your sister. If that's true, I'm not sure what to tell you. You and your sister are as different as night and day."

"I didn't say I wanted to be like Deborah," Dee said. She didn't tell her mother she'd given up that fantasy years ago. "I just wonder if I could do something to make boys like me more."

She peered at Dee. "This doesn't sound like you. You're always right in the middle of things, doing as you please. This boy must be pretty special."

"Yeah," Dee said casually, trying to hide her feelings. "I guess he is."

"And he thinks you're too silly for him?"

"Something like that."

"Then maybe he's not the right boy for you."

Bantam Sweet Dreams Romances
Ask your bookseller for the books you have missed

Just The Way You Are

Janice Boies

BANTAM BOOKS

TORONTO • NEW YORK • LONDON • SYDNEY • AUCKLAND

To my father, for his
support and encouragement.

RL 6, IL age 11 and up

JUST THE WAY YOU ARE
A Bantam Book / December 1986

Cover photo by Pat Hill.

ISBN 0-553-25815-X

Published simultaneously in the United States and Canada

*Bantam Books are published by Bantam Books, Inc. Its trademark,
consisting of the words "Bantam Books" and the portrayal of
a rooster, is Registered in U.S. Patent and Trademark Office
and in other countries. Marca Registrada. Bantam Books, Inc.,
666 Fifth Avenue, New York, New York 10103.*

PRINTED IN THE UNITED STATES OF AMERICA

O   0 9 8 7 6 5 4 3 2 1

Just The Way You Are

Chapter One

"There he is," Dee whispered to herself.

She'd been wandering around the halls looking for Jeremy Griffin since the end of the sixth hour. Cupid's Arrow, the computerized love match service the Honor Society sponsored for Valentine's Day, had given Dee the most exciting news about Jeremy and her, and she wanted to find him to tell him about it.

No one would ever have called Dee Davidson shy. The best thing about her was that she was always able to laugh at her frequent disasters—and make other people laugh at them, too. But Jeremy Griffin was no laughing matter to Dee. Just the thought of him reduced her to a mass of quivering jelly.

He was always so cool, so together. He was tall and blond, first trumpet in the band, and the only person who had a picture of himself with the president of the United States taped to the

1

inside of his locker door. But Dee's friends couldn't understand why she was so interested in him; it wasn't as if they had anything in common. In fact, they'd never even met. Besides, Jeremy always acted a little—well, a little stuck-up, as if he were better than everybody else.

But that didn't matter. The only thing that mattered to Dee was getting a date with Jeremy. When her older, sophisticated sister, Deborah, had gone to Hill High, she had dated every important guy there—except for the two older Griffin brothers. She'd never been able to get so much as a second look from either of them. Well, now it was Dee's turn. She didn't have Deborah's looks or her ability to charm guys; at least, that was the way Deborah had always made her feel. But if it took all year, Dee was going to get the one thing that her sister hadn't gotten—a date with a Griffin. In this case, Jeremy Griffin.

But even thinking about introducing herself to Jeremy always turned Dee into a nervous wreck. The last time she'd considered walking up and starting a conversation with him, she'd sprained her ankle on the way! It hadn't really been her fault, though. Who'd have expected to find a puddle of water from a leaky drinking fountain around the corner from his locker? It wouldn't be like that now; this time she had something special to tell him—something that would make all her dreams come true!

Suddenly she saw him right ahead of her, standing in the center of the band hall with another guy. His trumpet case was sitting on the floor next to him, his books balanced on top. He looked terrific. No, not just terrific—perfect. That was it. Everything about Jeremy was perfect: his looks, his clothes, his posture—even the way he balanced his books on top of the trumpet case. She knew they wouldn't tumble to the floor. Jeremy Griffin's books wouldn't dare fall off.

Dee clutched the printout in one hand and ran the other through her short, brown curls. Taking a deep breath, she smoothed out her fluffy bangs. When they were lying just right, they made her eyes look bigger. She wanted to look her best for Jeremy.

She headed toward him, her heart pounding so loudly she was sure the sound would echo in the nearly empty hall; but the guys didn't seem to notice. Then she got close enough to hear part of their conversation.

"And I don't know why he bothered to challenge you. Everyone knows you're the best." By now Dee recognized Jeremy's deep-voiced friend as another band member. "You'll be first

3

trumpet until you graduate next year," he continued.

"I know," Jeremy agreed immodestly.

"Hi, Jeremy," Dee announced. Why did her voice sound so rough? she wondered. When she'd practiced the line in the restroom, it had sounded bouncy and confident.

Both heads turned to look at her. She pasted a big smile on her lips and tossed back her curls. "Guess what? You're my Number One."

His friend made a kind of choking sound, but Dee's attention was centered on Jeremy. His blue eyes were cold as he looked down at her. "What are you talking about?"

Dee had thought her opening line would make him curious, but he sounded bored—as if girls fed him lines like that every day. Still, Dee wouldn't let that worry her. She had proof! Offering him the Cupid's Arrow printout, she said, "It's right here in dot matrix. Jeremy Griffin is my number-one match with a compatibility rating of eighty-five."

He snatched the paper from her and tried to smooth out the crinkles so he could read it. She realized the folds would tell him she'd been carrying the sheet around in her damp, nervous hands all day. Luckily, he seemed to be too busy studying the figures to notice that the printout was full of creases. He squinted, and Dee had the

4

awful feeling that he was trying to convince himself it was all a joke—a not-so-funny joke.

"Is it true?" Jeremy's friend asked.

"Yeah." Jeremy looked from the paper to Dee, then stared at the list again.

His silence was making her really jumpy. And the expression on his face—well, there was no expression on his face!

"This really doesn't prove a thing," he told her bluntly. "Whoever programmed the computer could have made a mistake."

He was so curt and looked so cold that she was stunned. She'd known it wouldn't be easy to convince him the computer printout was absolute proof that they belonged together, but he hadn't even given her a chance to overwhelm him with her charms.

For once, Dee couldn't think of a single, funny thing to say. She decided it was time to leave and made a show of checking her watch. "Well, I've got to go. See you around, Jeremy."

She tossed her head once more before walking down the hall. It wasn't a bad retreat, she told herself, at least she hadn't cried.

After she turned the corner, Dee flattened herself against the wall and craned her neck so she could hear Jeremy's conversation with his friend. It was at times like these that she really appreciated being short and skinny. It was easy to hide.

"How'd you manage to show up on Davidson's list?" Jeremy's friend asked.

"How should I know?" Jeremy said. "It's probably something dumb like we both checked that we would rather eat pistachio fudge ice cream than shrimp pizza."

"Pistachio fudge? Why would you check that? You hate it."

"I know, but I checked it because Mary Beth Kramer loves it. She could eat it for breakfast, lunch, and dinner."

"Mary Beth Kramer? She's so quiet!"

"I know, that's what I like about her," Jeremy exclaimed. "Mary Beth is calm. Dee *is* cute, but she's so—so—"

"Yeah, I know what you mean. Don't you wonder what she thinks is so funny all the time? I bet if you blew into one of her ears, the air would come right out the other side."

Dee squared her shoulders indignantly. He was wrong! She might act crazy sometimes and have too many accidents, but she was *not* an airhead. She'd aced the surprise quiz in Ms. White's English class that very day—that *proved* her head couldn't be completely empty.

"And have you ever heard her laugh?" continued Jeremy's friend.

"Who hasn't?" Jeremy said with an odd, snorting noise. "Sounds like a flock of geese flying overhead."

Then there were footsteps, and Dee realized the guys were walking away. She scooted to the edge of the wall, listening hard.

"Davidson's just a loser," she heard Jeremy's friend say.

"I wouldn't say that." Jeremy's voice was getting fainter, and Dee strained to hear the rest of his comment. "A lot of us think she's cute. But you know how she acts—tripping over her own desk while the whole class laughs. Everybody still talks about the time she choked on applesauce in the cafeteria and had to be saved by the custodian's Heimlich maneuver. Applesauce! I want a girlfriend—not the sophomore class clown."

Dee listened to the boys laughing as they moved out of range. She blew the bangs off her forehead and chewed on her lip while she thought things over.

It was going to be harder than she had thought to get Jeremy Griffin to ask her for a date. At least he said he thought she was cute. The results of the Cupid's Arrow search should have made things easier—but, no. Things only went her way when she worked really hard to *make* them come her way, like winning the lead role in *West Side Story* the past summer at the community theater.

Well, Jeremy Griffin was worth the same kind of effort. She'd show him she could be a girlfriend and not the class clown.

Behind her, Dee heard something jingle and recognized the sound as her best friend's dangling earrings. Ever since Allison had cut her hair short, she had been wearing jewelry that looked like fishing tackle. But both the haircut and the earrings looked good on Allison, who was tall and slim.

"Hey, Dee, there you are. I was looking for you. What've you been doing since lunch?"

"I picked up my Cupid's Arrow results." Dee smiled and handed Allison the printout sheet. "See who's my Number One? I couldn't wait to tell Jeremy about it—"

"What'd he say?" Allison interrupted.

"He called me a clown. In fact, he was very cold."

Allison gave Dee's arm a comforting squeeze. "So why are you smiling?"

"Because I'm going to make him change his mind. You know how long I've wanted to get a date with him."

"All year. And all year I've tried to figure out *why*. Jeremy Griffin is boring, and you're such a fun person. What would you do with him? What in the world would you guys talk about? Why do you want him?"

"I—I don't know. I just do." Dee knew that wasn't the truth, and she wished she didn't have to lie to her best friend. But even Allison wouldn't understand that Jeremy was the most important part of her plan to compete with her older sister now that Deborah was away at college.

"I think I should get you out of here before you tackle Griffin and drag him into some dark corner. Come on—let's go to your locker and then head for home."

"How about you?" Dee asked as they started down the hall. "You signed up for Cupid's Arrow, too."

"Yeah, I know. Would you believe it? My list includes all seniors. What sophomore girl is going to call up some senior and say, 'You're on my list'?"

"You would," Dee said bluntly.

Allison laughed. "Maybe. But the guys on my list aren't worth it."

"We should have guessed that stupid match service sounded too good to be true. Ted Connors is even on my list."

"Ted? Your brother's best friend?" Allison stopped walking and looked at Dee thoughtfully. "Now that *is* interesting."

"What's so fascinating about a guy who practically lives at my house? He might as well be my second brother."

"I'd take Ted Connors for a brother any day. In case you haven't noticed, he's tall, dark, and handsome. And I've heard he's got a good chance to be the starting pitcher for the varsity baseball team this spring."

"Baseball? Not you, too! Ted and my brother are always hanging around the house talking pitching, fielding, and batting," Dee complained.

"Maybe you ought to forget your baseball phobia and take another look at Ted," Allison suggested.

Dee glanced at her friend. "I'll think about it, OK?"

"I heard about the singing telegram you delivered in Wilson's class," Allison said as they went down to the first floor.

"Yeah, that was pretty funny," Dee admitted. "It was a singing valentine for some freshman."

"I bet she wanted to crawl under her desk!" Allison said, laughing.

"She did kind of slump down in her chair and blush. Then I was late getting to chorus—I got my sleeve caught in my locker—"

"So what else is new?" Allison interrupted and rolled her eyes.

Dee nodded. "By the time I got there and

grabbed one of the cardboard heart crowns, all the ones in my size were gone. Mine kept slipping, and when I started to sing, it fell even more, until by the time I hit the last note, the crown was sitting on my nose. I couldn't see a thing, and I started to laugh."

"Oh, no!" Allison cried, whooping.

"You know me and my laugh. The class was nearly hysterical by the time I left."

Allison pointed to Dee's locker as they neared it. "What's that?"

Dee looked and saw something white sticking through the crack between the door and frame. "It's just a sheet of paper."

When they reached the locker, Dee could tell it was an envelope. She gave it a tug, but it was wedged tightly in the crack between the locker door and its frame. Dropping her books to the floor, she spun the dial. The door popped open and the envelope fell out.

Allison bent to pick it up. Her finger nudged the small rip in one corner. "See the red card inside? It's a valentine."

Dee took the envelope, wondering what kind of card was inside. For a moment she hesitated. Then she slipped her finger under the flap and tore it open.

When Dee pulled out the card, she and Allison both gasped. It was beautiful. The glossy front showed two people holding hands in the distance. The picture was hazy, as if it were part of a dream.

"I'm going to die if I open this up and it says, 'Roses are red, violets are blue,' " Dee said.

Allison nodded. "I know what you mean. But open it anyway."

Dee peeked inside. There was no printed poem, but the handwritten message sent a chill down her back. She let the card dangle from her fingertips and smiled dreamily into space, savoring her first romantic valentine.

"Let me see it." Allison grabbed the card from her friend and read aloud: " 'I want to be your stranger across a crowded room.' " She squinted at the words and then read them again to herself. "What's this stranger bit? It sounds weird to me."

"It's a line from 'Some Enchanted Evening,' a song in the play *South Pacific*. You know what this means, don't you?"

"The guy's from some foreign country?"

"Wrong. It means whoever sent this knows about me—and the way I love musicals."

"You think he knows you're trying out for *Oklahoma!*?"

Dee thought about it. "Maybe."

"Too bad he didn't sign the card," Allison said.

"He's not much good to you if you don't know who he is."

"Yeah, I know," Dee said and sighed. It had been some day. First Jeremy Griffin, the man of her dreams, had rejected her. Then she'd acquired a secret admirer. "So I'm right back where I was before—watching TV alone on Friday night."

"You never know," Allison told her. "It's only Tuesday. But if nothing better comes along, we could watch together."

"It's a deal." They shook hands.

Suddenly they heard voices and turned to look down the hall. Dee's brother, Daniel, and his sidekick, Ted, were heading straight for them. Quickly Dee stuffed the valentine into her notebook. If Daniel saw it, he'd tease her about it all day.

Her older brother looked the same as he always did; Dee hardly even glanced at him, except to notice that his letter jacket was hanging open. It was Ted she really looked at—almost as if she were seeing him for the first time.

His jacket was tossed over one shoulder, and the long sleeves on his knit shirt rippled over his muscles. He was in much better shape than her brother. Maybe it was because they had just been discussing him, but something seemed different about Ted right then. As the guys walked closer, Dee noticed the firm set of his jaw and the sparkle in his eyes.

"Did you have a good Valentine's Day?" Ted didn't seem to be addressing either Dee or Allison in particular, but Dee felt his gaze settle on her.

"OK."

"We've been looking for you," Daniel told her. "Do you want a ride home?"

Neither girl would turn down a ride. Only a few days before they had enjoyed a February thaw, but now the Minnesota winter winds were back in full force.

"Just let me get my stuff." Dee's books were resting on the floor where she'd dropped them. She used a foot to shove them out of her way, then reached for her jacket at the back of the locker.

"Careful, don't trip over those books," Daniel said, pretending to be concerned for his little sister's welfare.

Dee turned toward her brother, determined to keep an eye on him. It was hard to trust someone who put Softsoap on her toothbrush. She slipped one arm into a sleeve, and the jacket began swinging behind her. Out of habit, she leaned back to capture the other sleeve, but it swayed in the opposite direction. Still watching Daniel, she lunged to the right, blindly reaching for the loose sleeve until she bumped into something. An instant later, she was sitting on the floor next to Ted.

"What happened?" she asked in a daze.

"What usually happens?" her brother asked. "You fell over your own feet."

"I did not!"

Allison covered her mouth to smother her laughter.

"It was me," Ted broke in. "I was getting your books for you, and I got in your way."

"Hardly. You were being a gentleman—" Dee paused to see if Daniel had noticed she'd called his friend a *gentleman*. "And while you were being gallant, I tripped over you."

"Maybe you did," he agreed and began to chuckle.

She watched as he stood up with her books tucked under one of his arms. He offered his other hand to her, and she accepted. It was impossible not to notice Ted's warm brown eyes or his firm grip as he pulled her up. When she was on her feet, he handed over her books. Suddenly she noticed that her anonymous valentine had somehow slipped into view.

"Thanks," she said quickly, trying to slant the notebook so the card would slip back where it belonged. If she did something obvious, like stuffing it back inside, her brother would know she was trying to hide something.

"No problem . . ." Ted's voice faded, and Dee realized he was studying the card.

"I really appreciate it," she continued, trying to sound casual while she pushed the valentine out of sight. She sensed Ted was still watching her, so she tipped her head up to look up at him. He was blushing a little, but his eyes were serious. He looked as if he was getting ready to say something to her.

"You're welcome," he said finally and dropped his gaze to a spot on the floor near her feet.

"Time to go," Daniel announced, holding his fist to his mouth like a microphone. "That is, if you're in any condition to travel," he added to Dee.

Dee forgot about Ted's odd behavior as she resumed her ongoing battle with her brother. "Y'know, I don't think I tripped at all. I bet *you* pushed me!"

Chapter Two

"Why so quiet?" Daniel asked as he turned the car away from the curb. "Are you sick, Dee?"

Allison waved from her doorstep, and Dee raised a hand in her friend's direction before answering her brother. "I feel fine."

Daniel peered into the rearview mirror. "Your face is kind of green. You look lovesick to me."

"How would you know?" she shot back.

Ted leaned against the window in the front and turned to look at her with interest. At least he *seemed* interested.

"It's Jeremy Griffin, right."

"Who told you?"

"So I am right! You've got to give up this crazy fantasy about Jeremy Griffin. It wouldn't matter if you grew six inches and bleached your hair. He'd never notice you. If our perfect older sister couldn't get a date with either of Jeremy's older brothers, what makes you think you can change enough to convince a Griffin to date you?"

"Don't be so sure of yourself," Dee said softly.

"What are you going to do? Squeeze into Deborah's skintight jeans?"

"Of course not!" Dee cried, stung. "I can change in other ways." She honestly had no idea how she was going to get Jeremy, but her brother didn't need to know that.

She glanced at Ted and noticed that he looked worried. Maybe he was thinking really hard. Well, if that was the case, he was probably thinking about baseball.

When the car pulled into the Davidsons' driveway, Dee gathered her things slowly together before climbing out of the car. She was surprised when Ted opened the back door and held it for her. Still irritated, she tried to ignore the impulse to talk to him.

Gently he touched her arm. "Dee? Could you wait a minute?"

"I guess so," she said, looking up at him. She watched different expressions cross his face: first he looked as if he wanted to say something but decided not to, then he sighed and shook his head slightly. Dee was getting cold while she waited for him to do something.

"When do you try out for the play?" he asked at last.

"Friday afternoon." Why couldn't he have asked her that inside her warm house?

"Are you nervous?"

"Sure."

Then it was quiet again, except for a few passing cars.

"Daniel's birthday is next Tuesday. Are you doing anything about it?" Ted asked.

Finally she was beginning to understand what he was getting at. They could hardly talk about birthday plans in front of Daniel. "I want to really embarrass him, but I haven't decided how."

"Well, I've got some ideas. Want to *do* his locker with me?"

"That'd be great!" If anyone knew how to get Daniel, it would be Ted.

"Hey! You coming?" Daniel yelled to Ted from inside the house.

"Be right there," he called over his shoulder, then he stepped closer to Dee. He looked past her and spoke softly. "People like you the way you are. You don't have to change."

"Sure, most people like me. I make them laugh." Dee didn't know what Ted was trying to tell her and her feet were starting to freeze. While she waited for him to continue, she stamped to stop the tingling.

"That's not what I meant." Ted bent his head

and looked straight into her eyes. "Sure, some people like you because you cheer them up, but don't you know what a good friend you are? You care about people, and you know how to make them feel good, even when they don't want to."

Ted's compliments were embarrassing Dee. "Name one time I did something like that."

"Just yesterday when I came over to your house in the middle of dinner. You didn't know why I was there, but you got another plate out and shared your dessert."

Dee knew why Ted spent so much time at her house. His parents were busy with their careers, and they weren't home much. Since he was an only child, there was no one for him to talk to at night. All the Davidsons tried to be friendly to Ted. What was different about her sharing her cake?

"Thanks, but I don't think I did anything special."

"And that's what makes you a good person. Don't change. If Jeremy Griffin is too dumb to like you the way you are, then—"

"Then what?"

"Never mind." He turned and ran up the sidewalk to join her brother.

"Is something wrong, Dee?" her dad asked at the dinner table. She was glad he'd waited until

Daniel had disappeared before he'd started asking questions. "You look worried about something."

Worried? She was worried all right, trying to decide what to do next about Jeremy. Was Daniel right—should she change? Or should she keep trying to win Jeremy's attention by being herself, as Ted advised? And how was she supposed to explain the problem to her father?

"I guess it's something about a boy, isn't it?" he asked, trying not to prod.

"Yeah." She picked at the apple pie on her plate, not wanting to say any more. Maybe the whole thing would go away if she didn't talk about it.

"Well, what's the problem?"

Dee sighed. "He thinks I'm too silly for him."

"Silly?" her father boomed. "Nonsense. I wouldn't have you any other way. Who else would bake me banana bread for my birthday and use a cup of salt instead of sugar?"

"It was an accident," she reminded him.

"Of course it was. Just like the time you tried to shampoo the carpet with Prell."

"Dad, I was four years old when I did that."

"Doesn't matter," he insisted. "You're the only one of my children with a sense of humor, and I wouldn't trade you for anyone."

With that, he pushed back his chair and left

the room. Dee knew he was going to the den to read his paper.

"What about you?" Dee asked, turning to her mother.

Caroline Davidson began carrying dessert dishes to the sink, and Dee jumped up to help her.

"What are you asking me, Dee?" her mother asked as they rinsed plates. "It sounds as if you want to be more serious—more like your sister. If that's the case, I'm not sure what to tell you. You and your sister are as different as night and day."

"I didn't say I wanted to be like Deborah," Dee said. She didn't tell her mother that she'd given up that fantasy years ago. "I just wonder if I could do something to make boys like me more."

A glass slipped from her mother's hand, but she caught it before it hit the sink. She peered at Dee. "This doesn't sound like you. You're always right in the middle of things, doing as you please. This boy must be pretty special."

"Yeah," Dee said casually, trying to hide her feelings.

"And he thinks you're too silly for him?"

"Something like that." Dee fitted the dinner plates into the dishwasher.

"Then maybe he's not the right boy for you."

"Don't say that!" Dee cried. "There's got to be a

way I can get him to notice me." *For the right reasons,* she added silently. He'd already noticed her for the *wrong* reasons.

"Why don't you take some time to watch him with his friends? Try to learn something from them," her mother suggested.

"I guess I can do that." Her mother didn't know she'd already been watching Jeremy and his friends for six months. If it took her that long to find out that he thought she was the class clown, what good would it do to watch him for another week?

Her mom started humming a cheery little tune while she wiped the counter with a damp cloth, obviously believing she'd just solved another crisis in the Davidson family.

Dee didn't have the heart to show her she was wrong by asking more questions, so she flipped the dishwasher latch and wiped her hands on a towel. "I think I'll go tackle my homework. My teachers are piling on the work now that it's nearly spring break."

Upstairs, Dee settled herself at her desk, honestly planning to study. But every time she tried to concentrate the words would float across the page. The day's events kept running through her head. Faces and voices appeared from nowhere.

Jeremy's steely blue eyes stared back at her

from her history book and his cool voice said, "I want a girlfriend—not the class clown."

"You've got to give up this crazy fantasy about Jeremy Griffin," said Daniel.

"You and your sister are as different as night and day," her mother said.

"I wouldn't trade you for anyone." Her dad's promise made her feel warm inside, but it didn't help with her problem. Funny, but that was her father's approach to most problems: he loved life, he had a laugh that shook the house, and Dee loved him. But she knew better than to ask him any serious questions. What kind of advice could she expect from a man who thought it was cute to give all his children "double D" names—Deborah, Daniel, and Denise?

"You care about people . . ." Once again, Ted's kind words made her smile. Maybe she was wrong about him.

"I want to be your stranger across a crowded room," Dee whispered as she looked over her shoulder at the valentine, now taped to her mirror. She sighed. The odds that Jeremy was her stranger were a trillion to one.

"Well, Mr. Stranger," she said aloud, "where are you when I need you?"

She closed her history book and tried to start her English assignment. But when she looked at the paper, all she could see was Jeremy's face.

His sandy hair was short, showing off his perfect ears. His teeth were straight, and as far as she knew, he'd never worn braces. His nose was just right—not too long or curved up on the end like hers.

When she reached out to touch the image in her mind, the eyes grew cold. The perfect teeth flashed as he said, "I want a girlfriend—not the sophomore class clown."

Not again! Her brain had locked onto the phrase, like a bad record stuck on the worst cut of the album.

Stuffing the blank paper back into her folder, Dee set her books aside and, with a heavy sigh, rested her head on her arms. It was time for some serious thinking.

She knew she wasn't ready to give up on Jeremy Griffin. And maybe she should be glad she overheard his comments. Now at least she understood the problem. If she ever wanted to date him, she'd have to convince him there was nothing wrong with class clowns. How was she going to do that?

She tried to think of what made Jeremy laugh. That day he laughed when his friend had made fun of her. Dee had seen him chuckle at a guy in the cafeteria who had tripped and spilled his food. And Jeremy and his friends had nearly killed themselves laughing once when someone had directed a sophomore boy into the girls' locker room.

Dee was beginning to understand. It looked like Jeremy didn't have any trouble laughing at people who weren't as perfect as he was. Sure, she could make him laugh at her. But every time he smiled or chuckled over her disasters, he'd be telling himself she was not good enough for him. So from now on, the last thing she'd do was give Jeremy Griffin any reason to laugh at her. Daniel was right: she had to change. But how?

Dee frowned. Deborah had always been her idea of a successful woman. Guys fell all over themselves to get a date with her, but not the two older Griffin boys. They'd never been victims of her charms. So the trick was to remember how Deborah had gone about pursuing them, and then do a better job.

Dee had spent most of the last years ignoring her sister's coy smile, poise, and witty conversation. Deborah's face never broke out before a school dance. Deborah never tripped over her own feet—or anyone else's. Deborah always knew what to say in any situation. She'd have been the perfect girl for Jeremy.

Dee looked around the room, remembering how it had been before Deborah went to college in the fall. There had been an invisible line down the center of the bedroom, and Deborah's half had been decorated with ruffled pillows, stuffed animals, and pictures of the Hill High football team.

Now the football players were in Deborah's scrapbook, and the bedroom walls were covered with Dee's movie posters. The pillows and animals Deborah hadn't carted off to college were crammed inside her closet, along with the clothes she hadn't had room to take.

How would Deborah have tackled the Jeremy Griffin problem?

Dee jumped off the bed and walked around the room, searching for an answer. She threw open the door to Deborah's closet, slamming it against the wall. Rustling through the clothes, she came out with a fuzzy sweater in a dreamy pastel blue. Deborah had said boys couldn't help but want to touch such softness.

Holding the soft, blue sweater up in front of her, Dee crossed the room to her mirror. With the balloon sleeves from her own sweater sticking out, it was hard to tell how Deborah's top would look.

"Why not?" Dee asked herself with a mischievous grin.

She yanked her fuchsia sweater overhead and tossed it onto the bed. Then she slipped into Deborah's top and smoothed it nervously over her stomach. Afraid to look in the mirror, Dee closed her eyes and memories filled her head.

She'd been twelve the last time she'd tried to dress like Deborah. She had stolen her sister's new two-piece bathing suit and paraded into the living room, not realizing how ridiculous it looked on her flat body. Her father had laughed so hard that tears had run down his face. Dee had hammed it up, of course, and everyone had enjoyed it—even Deborah. But when she'd gone back to their room, Dee had promised herself she would never imitate Deborah again.

Now, taking a deep breath, she opened one eye and peeked. Unwilling to believe what she saw, Dee opened both eyes and looked again. "What do you know?" she murmured.

It didn't look too bad. Of course, the soft blue sweater had looked ten times better on Deborah. And Dee didn't have long blond hair falling softly over her shoulders.

But it was a start, she decided happily. She sniffed the air and breathed in a familiar scent. Lifting one arm to her nose, Dee recognized the smell. Lilac. Deborah always sprayed lilac cologne down her neck and up her wrists, and the flowery fragrance had lingered. It wasn't bad, but Dee would have to find a different cologne. Lilacs didn't appeal to her.

Dee sighed and slowly lifted Deborah's sweater

over her head. She was willing to consider wearing different clothes, she decided, maybe something more feminine than the loose shirts she usually wore. But it was going to take more than clothes to get Jeremy interested in her. How had Deborah dealt with the guys once she'd slipped into tight jeans and fuzzy sweaters?

Probably, Dee thought, her sister would have swayed up to Jeremy and asked in her honeyed voice, "Jeremy, did someone actually challenge you for the first trumpet position? How could anyone be so stupid?"

Forget it, she told herself. There had to be another way. It had always sounded cute when Deborah spoke lines like that in her silky voice, but it wouldn't sound the same coming from Dee. Her husky voice would trip over the words, and she'd end up laughing—which was the *last* thing she wanted!

Her mother was right. She could not *be* Deborah.

But Jeremy Griffin wanted a princess, someone like her sister. "What am I going to do?" she muttered to herself.

Pretending to be Deborah wasn't going to help her get Jeremy. And acting like herself had already failed. What other choices were there? Could she change something about her appearance or her behavior?

It had been a long time since Dee had thought about the way she acted. In grade school she had decided that if people were going to laugh at her, then she would make sure they laughed when she wanted them to. It wasn't fun being laughed at—but it wasn't bad when people laughed *with* her, when she decided on the joke. And once she'd made that decision, she hadn't given a second thought to the things she did and said.

Now Dee decided the time had come for her to take another look at herself. Jeremy obviously saw things he didn't like, and it was up to her to discover exactly what had made him call her a clown. That would be her first step in the win-Jeremy-Griffin-campaign. The next day she would try to see herself the way Jeremy saw her—she would pretend she was another person observing Dee Davidson.

"I can't wait," Dee murmured, growing excited. It was going to be fun!

Chapter Three

Dee skidded to a stop in front of her first hour English class. It was quiet inside, and she assumed Ms. White had called the class to order. Dee wasn't particularly worried, though. She'd been late so many times already—usually because of an accident—that the idea of facing her least favorite teacher didn't intimidate her.

Ms. White was pacing back and forth in front of the first row of desks, quizzing the class about the reading assignment from the day before. Immediately Dee saw there was no way she could get to her desk on the window side of the room without Ms. White seeing her. So, taking a deep breath, she strolled slowly toward the teacher.

"Dee's here, now we can get started," someone called from the back of the room.

"Am I late?" she asked, pretending she hadn't heard the bell ringing as she'd rushed through the hall.

"Class began five minutes ago," Ms. White said in her usual clipped tones.

"Sorry." Oversleeping really had been kind of an accident. But Dee didn't think Ms. White would agree, so she kept quiet about it. Dropping into her seat, she tried to catch her breath and gather her thoughts. The whole morning had been such a big hurry she hadn't had a chance to make plans for the day.

All evening, thoughts of Jeremy Griffin and how to win his attention kept going around and around in her brain. Her head had been spinning when she'd finally gone to bed, and she hadn't fallen asleep until after midnight. When the alarm rang, she had had a hard time waking up and for a minute thought it was Saturday. Then, when she had realized it was Wednesday, she raced for the bathroom and jumped into the shower. She hadn't even really dried off—just pulled on a pair of jeans and an oversized red sweater and rushed to school.

"Now that we've finished discussing yesterday's assignment, we're going to talk about using the library," Ms. White announced.

Dee groaned along with the others. Had she hurried to class only to be given a lecture on how to check out books from the school library? She leaned back against her chair, settling in for a boring hour. Suddenly her stomach muscles jumped—the unmistakable sign of approaching hiccups! *Just what I need*, she told herself.

Maybe if she kept her mind off them, they'd go away. She tried to concentrate on Ms. White's speech, something about a scavenger hunt in the library. To keep her hands busy, she ran her fingers backward through her hair. There had been only enough time to towel dry it, and she was worried the curls would dry flat. As her fingers lifted and separated the hairs, she felt a poke from behind.

"Cut it out," the boy behind her hissed.

She swallowed another hiccup and craned her neck to look at him. "What's your problem?"

"Your wet hair," he said, pointing to the drops of water on his notebook paper.

"Excu-u-use me," she whispered and turned back to her desk. Most people wouldn't care if their English notes got a little soggy, but she had to be sitting in front of a brain. She wondered what Jeremy Griffin would think if she dripped on his notes. *You don't want to know*, she told herself.

"Do you have a question, Dee?" Ms. White asked.

Everyone turned to look at her, and Dee felt another hiccup coming on. Frantic now, she held her breath for five seconds before daring to answer Ms. White. "No."

"Fine. On this hunt, each of you will have a list of facts to find. This project will be done on your own time—" The class groaned again. "But today we'll talk about the kinds of places you can expect to find the answers."

Dee began to think about the project as if it were a real treasure hunt. Maybe the answers would be hidden under the table legs. Or stuck to the bottom of the tape player in the listening room. As she imagined all the different possibilities, Dee started to giggle.

"Is there something you want to share with us, Miss Davidson?" the teacher inquired.

Why not? Dee asked herself. "Will these facts be hidden in the library?" she asked aloud. "Like behind the librarian's ear or something?"

The whole class caught on and began to suggest places that should be checked. Behind the magazine rack. Under the carpet. Pinned to the drapes.

"Did you ever consider looking inside books?" the teacher asked. "Where would you look to find Benjamin Franklin's birthday?"

Someone suggested calling his mother, and while everybody giggled Allison raised her hand. "An encyclopedia."

"That is one place." Ms. White went on to describe other books that collected facts on famous people.

"How would you find out what day of the week June fifteenth fell on in nineteen thirteen?" Everyone stared at Ms. White. "I'll try again. If you went back in time to June fifteenth, nineteen thirteen, what day would it be? Monday? Saturday?"

Dee knew she'd seen a chart with that information once. What had she been reading that would have something that useless? Suddenly she remembered and waved her hand overhead, calling out, "An alman-*hic*-ac."

"An almanac?" Ms. White repeated. "That's right. How did you know that, Dee?"

"I remembered seeing a bunch of calendars— *hic*—when I was trying to find out if *Oklahoma!*—*hic*—ever won a Tony or Oscar award."

"Did it?" the teacher asked. She ignored Dee's hiccups and glared at the class as they began to laugh—quietly at first, then louder and still louder with every hiccup.

"I don't know. *Hic!* I had to go eat dinner. *Hic!*" Dee could no longer pretend that what was happening wasn't funny. The more people laughed, the louder she hiccuped. Finally she decided it was time to stop fighting the situation. She grinned, then started to laugh, the squawking sound of her laughter rose above everything else.

"People!" Ms. White barked, her arms folded

tightly over her chest. "Settle down. And, Dee, go take care of yourself."

Suddenly remembering her plan not to make any more scenes, Dee tried to look respectable as she left the room. She bit her lip hard, but she couldn't stop the laughter immediately. Between the hiccups and the suppressed squawks, her shoulders were shaking as she crossed the room in front of Ms. White.

Outside the classroom, Dee headed for a drinking fountain and tried to drown her hiccups. Then, feeling totally waterlogged, she slumped against the cool cement wall. What had she done? she asked herself. That day she was supposed to sit back and watch herself quietly, not cause a scene. How had it happened? "And *why*?" she muttered aloud.

Dee shook her head slowly and shuffled back to class. She pretended to listen to Ms. White for the rest of the hour, but her thoughts were on Jeremy. He would have been disgusted by her behavior. Someone as perfect as Jeremy would never be late for school. He wouldn't shake his wet hair over another guy's desk. And he'd probably never hiccupped in his life.

It was a terrible thing to have to admit, but Jeremy might have been right when he'd called her a clown.

*　　*　　*

The English class fiasco was still on Dee's mind at lunchtime. She wasn't really hungry, and the food tasted like cardboard; she tried to eat, and couldn't. People got up and sat down next to her and across from her, but she didn't see them. Conversations were going on all around her, but she didn't hear them.

For three hours she'd been wondering how Deborah would have handled the situation in English class. She could have been late for class—there was no question about that. It had taken her sister so long to dress every morning that she was late at least twice a week. And, of course, Deborah would have simply smiled her way into class.

Deborah had never left the house without her hair dry and shining, but what would have happened if she had? Dee tried to imagine the scene. If water from her sister's herbal-scented hair had spotted the brain's paper, he'd have been speechless. He might still have hated it, but he wouldn't have said anything. After class, some other guy probably would have tried to buy the paper from him! But not Dee's drips—they weren't worth anything.

And then there were the hiccups. She knew Deborah *did* get hiccups once or twice a year, but they were dainty little sounds that few people noticed. Still, at least, it proved her sister was human.

Dee sighed heavily. Jeremy had been right to laugh at the idea of having her as his girlfriend. It *was* pretty ridiculous. Viciously, she stabbed an overcooked green bean, looked at it as if it were a bug under a microscope, then made a face and put it back on her plate. She decided she'd finish off the applesauce and forget about the rest of her lunch.

Just as she dipped her spoon into the bowl, something came flying at her from the next table. It looked like a green bean. The mushed vegetable hit Dee's cheek and slid down the side of her face. Automatically, without thinking, Dee launched the applesauce on her spoon toward the attacker.

As she wiped her cheek, she saw the second round of beans coming toward her and ducked.

"Food fight!" someone screamed from the next table.

Dee sat up, wondering if she should toss her dish of green beans at the guy or just leave. She was making up her mind when she glanced toward the door and saw Jeremy walk into the cafeteria. There was no choice now. Dee crawled under the table, prepared to stay there all day if she had to.

*   *   *

"What's wrong with you, Dee Davidson?" Allison asked as they walked home together that afternoon. "You look terrible."

"That makes me feel much better," Dee grumbled, trudging along at her friend's side.

"Sorry. Are you going to tell me about your problem?" Allison stopped in the middle of the sidewalk and pulled her collar up to her chin.

"Yes, but I'm not going to stand out here in the wind to discuss it. Keep walking." Dee waited for Allison to start moving again. "Today I tried to see myself through Jeremy's eyes."

"And how'd you look?"

"Like a clown."

Allison's eyebrows shot up and she turned to Dee. "I thought you were kidding about *looking through* Jeremy's eyes. What'd you do today that was so terrible?"

"You saw the show I put on in English," Dee said with a shrug.

"I thought it was funny," Allison said, smiling again when she thought about it. "I haven't laughed that hard in English all year."

"Me, neither. But that's the problem. I can't seem to keep out of trouble, you know?" Dee said and heaved a huge sigh.

"But you didn't mean to get hiccups any more than you planned to get in a food fight at lunch."

"I don't *plan* to do a lot of things, but when I

39

get into certain situations, I do things that Jeremy Griffin and his friends wouldn't do. Can you imagine him slinging applesauce across the lunchroom?"

Allison shook her head. "Don't be so touchy about what Jeremy would and wouldn't do. Mr. Perfect would rather die than sneeze in class. Why would you want to be like him?"

"I don't want to be *like* him. I want *him* to like *me*!"

"OK, OK! You want him to like you. We both know that, but what's looking through his eyes going to do?" Allison was obviously losing her patience.

"I want to think the way I think *he* thinks. Then I'll be able to see what he doesn't like about me," Dee said proudly.

"And what have you discovered he doesn't like?"

"The way I deliberately try to get laughs."

It hurt to say that. Dee knew she liked being in charge, knowing people were laughing because she wanted them to. It seemed as if she always had to make people smile and giggle. She didn't know any other way to deal with her friends and family.

"I don't understand," Allison said quietly.

"I play up to the class," Dee explained. When her friend still looked lost, she went on, "Don't

40

you see? I could have excused myself the first time I felt a 'hic' coming on. And I didn't have to react when I got a green bean in the face. But I can't help myself. Wherever I am, things always happen, and I'm always involved. How could Jeremy ever want someone like that?"

"Maybe that's Jeremy's problem, and not yours," Allison suggested. "I don't want you to change."

"I *have* to change," Dee told her firmly. "After I saw myself today as Jeremy would, I can't go back to school and act that way again."

Dee didn't say anything about her plan for a new Dee. She'd been working on it since lunch, but it was still too new to share. Instead, they talked about other things, like how ridiculous it was to have to read fifty pages of history by the next day. They reached Allison's house first, and Dee hurried home alone.

She walked into her house and immediately called to her mother, "Could I have the car this afternoon?"

"Where did you want to go?" asked Mrs. Davidson, walking into the living room from her bedroom.

"I just have a little shopping to do," Dee said vaguely.

"Daniel has a dentist's appointment. Maybe he could drop you off somewhere."

41

"No way." Dee had big plans for the afternoon. She still had her Christmas money, and she'd been saving baby-sitting money since then, too. She was glad that she hadn't been able to decide how to spend it. She knew Daniel wouldn't wait for her while she shopped. And if he dropped her off at the mall, he'd probably forget to pick her up.

"I'll take you," Ted offered from the kitchen. "Daniel's left already. I've got my dad's car because he's out of town again."

Dee walked into the kitchen and noticed he'd helped himself to a piece of cake. "Would you do that?"

"Sure. Where do you need to go?"

"To the mall. I need lots of little things—to make a big change."

"A change?" Ted's eyes looked worried. "I hope you won't change too much. Remember what I said yesterday. People like you the way you are."

Dee decided that she understood what Ted was saying. People liked her the way she was because she made them laugh. She bristled inside. Was that why he didn't want her to change? Did he really want her to remain the sophomore class clown?

Well, she was tired of entertaining the whole school! She didn't care if "people" liked her the way she was. Dee only wanted one person to like her—Jeremy Griffin.

Chapter Four

"Morning," Mr. Davidson mumbled, barely glancing up from his toast and coffee. Then his head snapped up for another look. "Caroline, would you look at this?"

Dee's mother turned from the sink, where she was mixing juice. First she looked at Dee's smooth hairstyle, and then her gaze moved down to her soft shirt. "You look very nice."

"What's the event, Dee?" asked her father.

"Nothing special. And please don't call me 'Dee' anymore. My name is Denise," she said with more confidence than she felt.

"I know it is, but you're still Dee to all of us," her father said warmly and took a sip of his coffee.

"Dear, she's saying she *wants* us to call her Denise," her mother said gently.

"Denise" appreciated her mother's support, especially since she'd gotten up an hour early to

44

transform Dee Davidson into a new person. And it hadn't been easy. She'd squinted into the bathroom mirror, not sure the world really existed that early in the morning. But it did. Her favorite deejay was playing records and telling jokes by the time she'd stepped out of the shower.

She'd dusted her body with powder, then gasped for air as delicately scented clouds swirled all around her. It made her glad she'd chosen something that smelled light, like a spring garden, instead of Deborah's sickeningly sweet lilac fragrance.

It had taken forever to smooth out her wild curls with the blow dryer. Dee had wondered if her arm would fall off from being bent at the same angle for so long. But when she had looked into the mirror, she decided it was worth the effort. Now her brown hair framed her face with soft waves.

The V-necked pumpkin-colored top she'd bought the day before looked great with her brown-striped jeans. It had taken her fifteen minutes to twist and tie the brown scarf around her bare neck. Dee had picked up plenty of tricks with scarves and jewelry from Deborah.

The colors looked great on her. The pumpkin top gave her cheeks a natural blush, and the brown scarf made her eyes look bigger and darker. It surprised Dee to see how different she looked with new clothes. Of course, she had to do more than look different.

She was able to eat her breakfast in peace. Her father rushed off to work, and her mother was smart enough not to ask a lot of questions. When she finished her cereal, she rinsed the bowl in the sink and turned to her mother. "I'll be home a little late today," she said. "I want to listen to auditions."

"I thought you didn't try out until tomorrow," her mother said as she gathered together some bills and her checkbook.

"I don't. They're auditioning dancers today. But watching other people survive tryouts keeps me from getting too nervous."

"I'm sure you'll do fine tomorrow."

"I think so, too," she said confidently. Dee wasn't being vain; she knew her voice was strong and good.

As she opened the front door, her mother said, "Denise, I hope you have a very good day."

Dee grinned as she closed the front door behind her. She'd known she could count on her mom for support. On the way to school she thought about how she planned to act during the day. There would be no jokes—and *no* disasters! She would think before she opened her mouth or walked into a room. She would be too organized to have any accidents creep into her life.

Dee breezed into Hill High with plenty of time to get to class, but she caused quite a stir, in spite of her decision to stay out of the limelight. People turned to gape at her. Others tripped over the ones who had stopped to stare. It was a once-in-a-lifetime opportunity for *Dee* to make a scene, but Denise just smiled and said, "Good morning," to everyone.

She was the first person in her English class. Remembering that she hadn't finished her history assignment, she opened the thick book and started to read.

"Good morning, Dee," Ms. White said as her high heels clicked across the floor.

"If you don't mind—" she replied politely, looking up from her book—"could you call me Denise?" Ms. White's eyes narrowed as if she were trying to figure out what new game Dee was playing. "It's no joke," Dee assured her.

"All right," Ms. White said slowly, obviously still waiting for the punch line.

As her classmates drifted into English, each one looked at Denise. Some sat down and openly stared. Others pretended to talk or read, but kept peeking in her direction. Dee had spent a lot of time working out her plan to become

"Denise," but she hadn't anticipated all the interest the change would create.

At the last minute Allison rushed into the room. She blinked when she saw Denise. "What happened to you, Dee?" she called out to her friend before sitting down. "Oh, I know."

That statement made everyone even more curious, and the whole classroom was buzzing with questions. Meanwhile, Dee was having a hard time staying calm. Part of her wanted to grin and announce that she was suffering from a split personality—she was half Dee Davidson and half Mary Beth Kramer. She knew it would be guaranteed to get a laugh. However, her brain reminded her that she hadn't worked so hard and gone to so much trouble just to blow it over one joke. So she stared straight ahead and tried not to listen to what was being said.

Ms. White asked the class how the scavenger hunt was going. Everyone groaned. Then she announced they were starting a unit on current music that had been influenced or inspired by classical literature, art, and plays. She asked the class for examples.

Most of the students gazed at the teacher with glassy eyes, but Dee knew exactly what Ms. White was talking about. And it must have shown on her face.

"Dee—I mean, Denise, could you give us an

example of a play that is based on classical literature?"

"Who's Denise?" Heads turned and the question hummed from a dozen lips.

She looked directly at Ms. White, ignoring all the questions. "*West Side Story* is an example. It's a modern version of *Romeo and Juliet*."

Two guys made kissing sounds, and Dee realized they had been doing that every time someone mentioned anything romantic since the sixth grade. Funny that she'd never noticed how silly they sounded.

The room grew very quiet, and the back of Denise's neck prickled. People were waiting for something. She sensed it. Suddenly she knew what they wanted. They were expecting her to do something funny, like break into a quick verse of "I Feel Pretty."

Most of her classmates had seen her play Maria in the community-theater production of *West Side Story*. In January when Ms. White had mentioned the play, *Dee* had treated the class to the first verse and chorus, her voice growing stronger with each line.

It was tempting all right. The words were on the tip of her tongue; all she had to do was open her mouth and—but Denise kept her mouth firmly closed. Her friends could wait all hour; she wasn't going to sing. She looked at Ms.

White, hoping the teacher realized she wasn't trying to disrupt the class this time. Ms. White offered a reassuring smile and nodded.

"That's a good example, Denise. Thank you. Who can think of another one?"

Dee slumped back in her chair and let a little smile brighten the serious expression on her face. She'd done it! The old Dee Davidson had tempted her, but Denise had won.

Allison was waiting on the Davidsons' living room couch when Dee hurried into the house that afternoon.

"What's going on with you?" Allison demanded.

"Life is wonderful!" Dee exclaimed. "I'm ready to try out for the play tomorrow, and—"

"I don't want to hear about the play. I want to know about Denise," Allison interrupted.

"OK, but I have other news first. And you'll never guess what it is."

Allison sat back against the cushions with her arms folded stubbornly across her chest. "I don't want to guess."

"Then don't," Dee replied cheerfully, dropping onto the couch next to her friend. "After school I was walking from my locker to the auditorium, and Jeremy was walking the other way—"

"And he threw himself at your feet and begged

you to go out with him tomorrow night," Allison finished sarcastically.

"Not exactly." Dee was having a great time watching the look in Allison's eyes. She knew her friend didn't think Jeremy would ever notice her. "He passed me, then backed up to look at me. He blinked and said, '*Denise?*' "

"Then what happened?" Allison was hooked now; Dee could tell by her voice.

"I said, 'yes,' but my voice cracked because I was so nervous. He kind of shook his head at that and said, 'I'd heard you were different today,' and then he left."

"That's all?" her friend asked, obviously disappointed.

"It's a start. After just one day, he noticed me."

"In case you can't tell, he wasn't exactly complimentary," Allison pointed out.

"But he wasn't calling me a clown, either. Come on, Allison—I have to be positive about this."

"Whatever you say, Dee," said Allison, shaking her head.

"Please, call me Denise."

"Denise?" Just as Allison repeated the name in a doubtful tone of voice, Daniel and Ted passed through the living room. They both stopped and peered at Dee. Daniel made a face, but Ted seemed quite interested in her new appearance.

"What happened to you?" Daniel asked in his usual big-brother tone.

"You sound like I grew antennas overnight," Denise complained.

"It's more like you grew a whole new body," he said, leaning back and squinting. "Is that Deborah's shirt?"

"No," she snapped. "I bought it yesterday."

Daniel looked ready to start a fight, but Ted jumped into the conversation. "That's right. I was with her. And it looks very nice on you—Denise."

The guys shuffled off to Daniel's room, and Allison acted as if she couldn't wait for them to disappear. Eyes sparkling, she turned to Dee and said, "Ted took you shopping yesterday? That's wild! You know, he's more your type, I think."

"Be serious," Dee answered. "He took me shopping because Daniel needed our car to go to the dentist. Ted didn't have anything better to do."

"If you say so," Allison replied, trying to sound mysterious.

Dee couldn't tell if Allison really thought Ted was a great guy, but she decided she didn't really care. Probably her friend was just trying to find some competition for Jeremy. Allison looked as if she were about to say something else about Ted, but Dee distracted her. It wasn't hard to do—they hadn't been friends for four long years for nothing!

"I got some new eye shadow yesterday. Will you help me with it? I can't figure out which color should go in the crease, and which one belongs on the eyelid."

"A slap of shadow was good enough for you before. Is this for Jeremy, too?"

"Might be. Or it might be for my auditions tomorrow. I don't want to look pasty up on the stage."

"That's true," Allison agreed, smiling. She stood up. "OK, let's do it, Dee—Denise."

"Denise" attracted less attention the next day. People were already getting used to her new look. The soft, apricot-colored sweater she wore that day was feminine and cuddly. Following Allison's advice, Dee had carefully applied peach shadow over each eye, with just a trace under her lower lashes. She was going to glow on stage after school.

After lunch Dee left the cafeteria with her friends, fingering the smooth beads of a necklace Deborah had left at home.

The group wandered into the student lounge,

where they sat around until classes started. Just inside the door, Denise noticed Jeremy. He was sitting at a table with a sign that said, "Buy a candy bar to send the band on tour."

She considered buying a bar just to have an excuse to talk with him. After all, he had said something almost decent to her the day before. Then she remembered his cold voice saying, "You know what kind of girl she is . . ." Dee shook her head. Only a fool would give him a chance to say something like that in front of all her friends. And Denise Davidson was not a fool.

"Denise?"

Was that Jeremy calling her? Dee's heart jumped wildly in her chest, and she told herself she was imagining things. She lagged behind the group and dipped her head, pretending to look for a note or something in her history book. When she thought it was safe, she peeked up to check him out. Maybe it was cowardly, but it was better than staring at him.

"Please, come over and talk to me." It *was* Jeremy—and he sounded friendly!

"Me?" She mouthed the word and pointed at herself. True, he was looking at her when he said it, but Dee was sure he had to be talking to someone else.

"Yes, Denise. You."

By now her friends were at the other end of the

lounge. Someone had a radio, and rock music was drifting across the room. She glanced at the group and knew they wouldn't miss her.

Slowly she moved toward Jeremy, wondering why he'd called her over. She guessed he was bored since no one was buying any candy. After her outburst over the Cupid's Arrow report, he was probably feeling pretty confident that she would talk to him whenever he snapped his fingers.

He probably thought she'd do anything to get his attention. Well, Dee might, but not Denise. Denise wanted a date with Jeremy Griffin, but she wouldn't pull any crazy stunts to get one.

She leaned against the edge of the table and tried to smile at him. For the first time in years, her lips didn't curve into an automatic grin. She was too nervous to smile naturally. It felt as if her lips were sticking to her teeth. *Great impression you're making,* she told herself.

"You look very nice today," he said. "Yesterday, too."

"Thank you."

"Is there some reason—"

"When is the band going on tour?" she interrupted. The confident expression on Jeremy's face gave him away. He expected her to admit that she'd gone to all this trouble for him! Well, she wasn't about to admit that, so she wouldn't give him a chance to ask the question. Deborah, she knew, would have answered with a mysterious smile. Dee had tried to practice that look in her mirror last night, but she'd ended up looking like she had a stomachache.

The old Dee would have had dozens of answers. She could have described the aliens that had invaded her home and carried off all her bright, floppy sweaters. Or she could have explained that none of her clothes were new, that she'd simply shrunk all her oversized sweaters in the clothes dryer.

Yes, the old Dee had had an answer for every question. But unable now to fall back on her usual tricks, Denise was uncomfortable. Luckily, Jeremy didn't seem to notice.

"The band tour?" he repeated. "We're going to Disney World over spring break."

"That's less than a month away. You must be excited." Denise cringed. *Brilliant*, she thought miserably. Did Jeremy Griffin really get "excited" over things like band tours?

"We're all looking forward to it. We've been practicing hard, and now we're trying to sell the last of our candy bars."

"Should I buy one?" she asked, forcing a flirtatious smile to her lips.

He didn't seem to notice. "Only if you want to. I didn't invite you over here just so I could twist your arm." He smiled at his own brief attempt at humor. Or could he—just possibly—be returning her own smile? "I just wanted to talk to you a little."

Denise felt her stomach doing double somersaults. She wanted to shake her head to clear it and then ask him to say it again, to make sure she'd heard him correctly. Instead, she thought hard about the way Deborah would react in this kind of situation and said simply, "Really?"

Jeremy looked up at her with the light of approval in his eyes. Dee wondered if he'd thought she might do backflips over his admission.

"Have you tried out for the play yet?" he asked.

"*Oklahoma!?*" As soon as she said it, Dee wanted to sink right through the floor. Great reply, Denise, she told herself. What other play was the drama club putting on in the spring? "I'm auditioning this afternoon. Will you be in the orchestra?"

"I won't be able to be there. I have an appointment. I'm sure you'll get a part," he said generously. "I've heard you sing, and you've got a great voice."

He'd heard her sing? And remembered it well enough to have an opinion of it? Dee couldn't have been more stunned if he had invited her to the prom.

"What part do you want?" he asked. He seemed really interested.

Someone turned up the volume on the radio across the room. Dee heard the introductory bars to the latest Pointer Sisters song. It had a great beat, and her foot started to tap in time with the rhythm. She knew the rest of her body would start to sway any minute. Firmly, she made herself stop tapping.

Allison was standing on tiptoe, searching the room. Dee knew whom she was trying to find. She and Allison were considered the school's answer to the Pointer Sisters. Whenever their songs were played on the radio, the two girls sang along—as loudly as they could. With Dee singing the lead and Allison handling the harmony, they drowned out the radio each and every time. It was great fun, for the girls *and* their always enthusiastic audience. But Allison wasn't going to find her partner that day. Dee would see to that.

"Where's Dee?" she heard one of the guys call.

"Is someone looking for you?" Jeremy asked as he watched the scene across the room with moderate interest.

Without as much as blinking an eye, Denise answered, "No. What were you saying?"

"I asked which part you're hoping to get in *Oklahoma!*?"

"Laurie." Laurie was the lead role, and Dee hadn't even *thought* about trying out for it. Somehow it had just popped out.

"Good." The bell rang, warning them lunch period was nearly over. Jeremy started to gather up his money and the remaining candy bars.

Dee knew her next class was at the other end of the building, and she also knew that Denise couldn't be late, but still she hated to leave Jeremy. The last few minutes had been magical, almost too wonderful to be true. What if this were her only chance with Jeremy? What if he never spoke to her again? Finally she decided it was a risk she'd just have to take. She turned toward the door, then looked back and smiled brightly.

"Bye, Jeremy."

He closed the money box, and Dee heard loose change jingle when he looked up at her. "See you around. And break a leg this afternoon."

Dee avoided her friends on the way to class. She needed time to think. Jeremy Griffin had actually called her over to his table, talked to her, and finally said he would see her around. She was happy about it—but not so delirious as she believed she *should* feel. She couldn't understand it—a week ago she would have fainted at his feet if he had said those things.

And why had she told that lie about wanting

the part of Laurie? She had always planned to try out for Ado Annie, the second lead. Jeremy wouldn't know she hadn't been truthful, of course. He probably thought every girl would want the lead role. After all, would Jeremy Griffin ever settle for anything less than first trumpet? It might not cross his mind that some girls would prefer the show-stopping songs that Ado Annie got to sing.

Dee was glad Jeremy wouldn't be coming to the auditions. Anyone listening to her try out would know which role she was after. If Denise Davidson really wanted the part of sweet, feminine Laurie, would she be trying out with a loud, bouncy version of "Footloose"?

Chapter Five

"Why are Mondays always so hard?" Allison asked Dee as the lunchroom volunteer heaped corn on their plates. "I'm tired."

"Me, too," Dee agreed. She'd gotten up early again to blow dry her hair. Her new image was exhausting her.

As she followed Allison from the cafeteria line to the lunchroom, she felt a tap on her shoulder. Dee looked back and blinked in surprise.

"Jeremy?"

"Hi, Denise. Would you like to sit with me?"

Would she like to sit with him? That was like asking if she'd like to win ten thousand dollars. There was nothing she wanted more than to sit with Jeremy! She nodded and managed to say calmly, "Sure."

He took her elbow with his left hand and steered her to his table. His friends looked up and their mouths fell open, then quickly snapped shut again. She could see they were trying not to look too curious. But they needn't have tried to cover their shock. They couldn't have been any more surprised than she was.

Jeremy stopped before two empty seats. A lunch tray was sitting in front of one spot, and Denise figured it belonged to Jeremy. A notebook was resting on the other seat. Did that mean he'd been saving her a seat? Had he been watching for her?

He reached for her tray and held it while she sat down. When she looked up at him, their eyes met, and he smiled as he set the tray in front of her. Dee tried to smile back, but her face felt as if it was frozen in place—probably from the shock of being with him, she decided.

"Hello, Dee," said a grim-faced blond across the table. Dee looked up and recognized the guy who'd been with Jeremy during the Valentine's Day disaster.

"She prefers to be called Denise," Jeremy announced before she could reply.

"Sorry." The blond held out his hand. "I'm Alex."

Dee reached up to shake hands and knocked her fork off her plate. It bounced once and then clattered onto the table. Out of the corner of her eye, she saw Jeremy pick up the fork and balance it over her plate.

"Thank you," she murmured. *Watch it!* she warned herself. You may have gotten an invitation to sit at Jeremy's table, but you'll have to be careful if you want to stay here. People didn't drop their dishes or get into food fights in this crowd.

"As I was saying before you left," the blond said, picking up an earlier conversation with Jeremy, "you'll have the band vote, and the smart kids will vote for you, too, unless they put up their own candidate."

Dee frowned slightly and bit into her pizza-burger. What was Alex talking about? It sounded like Jeremy was planning to run for some office. But which one? No elections were held in the spring. There were positions like track or baseball captain, but she knew Jeremy didn't play baseball. And the band vote wouldn't make any difference on the track team.

"You'll need an issue. How about more parking spaces for students?" suggested the redhead sitting next to Alex.

"Or better funding from the school board for after-school activities?" said the skinny boy on Dee's other side.

"Those are *big* enough," Alex agreed. "Senior class president is an important job. It'll take a strong campaign—"

Senior class president? The seniors already

had a president. And besides, Jeremy was a junior. Then, suddenly, Denise realized Jeremy was plotting his strategy for next fall's elections.

She knew she ought to be impressed. She tried to imagine what it would feel like to be dating the senior class president next year, but somehow she just couldn't get excited. The Dee part of her kept asking what kind of high school student needed six months to win a class election.

Denise wanted to shrug off Dee's doubts. She had never run in an important election, so what did she know about it? Maybe it did take half a year to plan a successful strategy. U.S. presidential candidates spent more time than that on their campaigns—they started at least a year in advance.

But they were hoping to run the whole country, Dee pointed out, not the senior class at Hill High.

She interrupted her argument with herself long enough to watch Jeremy as he discussed his plans; his face was animated and his blue eyes sparkled. Dee could tell he loved politics. It was hard to believe those same eyes could turn cold and insulting, but she knew it was possible. She'd seen it. She would never forget it.

Although she was listening to Jeremy, two questions kept buzzing around in her head.

Why had Jeremy called her over to talk to him in the lounge the last Friday? And why had he invited her to share his table? She was dying to ask him but didn't know how to phrase the question, especially in front of his friends. Trying to picture Deborah in this situation was useless. Her sister would never have wondered why a boy like Jeremy wanted to spend time with her, so it would never have crossed her mind to ask him why he'd chosen her.

"Denise," someone whispered in her ear.

Jeremy's attention was on the presidential conversation, so Dee turned toward the mellow voice. Ted was kneeling behind her. "Hi," she said softly.

"Remember what day it is tomorrow?" he whispered.

"Tuesday?" she guessed.

"Daniel's birthday," he said, staring thoughtfully at Jeremy's back. "You said you wanted to help decorate your brother's locker before school. Are you still up for it?"

Of course she was still up for it! What was he talking about? Then she remembered. Jeremy. Would he and his friends do that sort of thing? It was hard to imagine them getting wrapped up in crepe paper as they looped and tied it over a locker.

She bit her lower lip, trying to decide if it

would be safe to join Ted in the morning. Things were just starting to happen with Jeremy, and she would hate herself if she blew it by doing something stupid. But Daniel was her brother, the guy who made her life miserable. How could she pass up a chance to pay him back, even a little? And so what if Jeremy wouldn't do something like that? He'd never know.

Leaning behind Jeremy's shoulder, she whispered, "I'll be there. What time?"

Ted bent closer; Dee could tell he understood she didn't want anyone else to hear their conversation. "Seven-fifteen. You're in charge of the balloons. Got it?"

"Yes, sir."

He took a deep breath, and she watched his eyes widen. "Is it you who smells so good?"

"It must be. It can't be any of these guys!" she answered with a grin.

Ted laughed and hurried off to find his friends. Dee looked quickly at Jeremy and the other guys. No one seemed to have noticed her conversation with Ted. Still, she was amazed at herself. What had made her risk joking with Ted behind Jeremy's back?

She had to admit, she enjoyed Ted's flattery. He'd been the first guy to notice her cologne. It seemed as if Ted was always among the first to compliment her whenever she did anything interesting.

Just then Jeremy wadded up his napkin, dropped it on his plate, and turned to her. "Ready to go, Denise?"

She looked at her empty dish and wondered where they were going. "Sure."

He picked up her tray and stacked it on top of his, then dropped them off on the conveyor belt. "Let's talk," he suggested.

Dee followed him to the empty band hall. Jeremy leaned casually against the wall, and she stood next to him, her hands stuffed in her jeans pockets to keep them from fluttering around like two escaped birds.

"How was your audition on Friday?" he asked.

"I don't know," she told him. She slid her hands out of her pockets, then decided to hook her thumbs back inside for safety's sake. "A lot of good singers tried out. Since I'm a sophomore, this is my first year with Martin. I couldn't tell what he thought of me, but he seemed to like some of the other girls."

Jeremy listened attentively. "When will you know?"

"The callback sheet will be posted tomorrow. If I make it, I'll have to audition again Wednesday."

"Well, I hope you're on the list," he said as people started filing into the band room.

"Me, too, Jeremy." Dee took a deep breath and stood looking at him.

"Well, Denise, until you showed me the Cupid's Arrow printout, I had never really noticed you before, and I'm glad you did show it to me. I was pretty rude that day, and I'm sorry."

"It's OK," Dee managed to say. Inside, she was stunned. An apology was the last thing she'd expected from him.

"To be honest, you seem different. Can you tell me why?"

Jeremy's slightly smug smile told Dee he figured *he* was the reason for all the changes. Well, she told herself, she wasn't going to feed his ego and admit that she'd done it for him. Still, she felt she owed him some kind of reply.

But as she searched for an excuse to explain her behavior, Denise discovered that the motivation for her experiment seemed to be more involved than just attracting Jeremy Griffin's attention. "I wanted to see if people would still like me if I wasn't always trying to entertain them," she told him slowly.

"Do they?"

"I haven't lost any friends yet."

"You've even found some new ones." He smiled down at her, flashing his perfectly even white teeth. "Would you like to go to a movie with me Friday night?"

Dee tried to act casual, as if his asking her out weren't the most important accomplishment of her high school career. But she couldn't do it. She knew she was staring at him, and she had to remind herself to breathe.

"Yes," she said, almost as a croak.

It had happened!

"Hey, Ted," Dee called, her morning voice echoing in the empty hall. Feeling slightly like a pack horse, she adjusted the strap on her shoulder. She hadn't worn a backpack all year, but it was the only way she could get everything to school that day.

Ted was waiting next to Daniel's locker. "What?" he managed to say before breaking into laughter. He pointed to the black plastic lawn bag slung over Denise's shoulder. "Are those the balloons?"

"Two and a half dozen," she said, nodding. "I was up half the night blowing into the little devils."

"You blew them all up?"

"Sure did," she replied proudly, slipping the backpack off her shoulders before setting it on the floor. "And I've got the sore cheeks to prove it. I must have puffed all night. Every time I smile or pucker, the inside of my mouth hurts."

"But, Dee—I mean, Denise, I asked you to be here early so we could blow them up together."

"Oh. I thought it would be fun my way."

He grinned again when she swung the bag off her shoulder and set it on the floor at his feet. The balloons inside kept shifting around, and it looked as if something were alive under the plastic. "You might be right."

She'd enjoyed sneaking the plastic lawn bag out of the house under Daniel's nose. Still, the thought of standing next to Ted while they both puffed themselves breathless made her heart beat faster. Dee told herself she was just excited about doing something crazy, something the old *Dee* used to do. She could be herself, without worrying that Jeremy might be around the corner. That's all it was. There couldn't be any other explanation—could there?

Ted twirled the locker dial with his fingers, and the door swung open on the first try.

"Good work. Do you break into lockers often?" she asked teasingly.

"The only combination I know is Daniel's. For example, I couldn't open yours."

"How do you know? Have you tried?"

Ted seemed to be avoiding her eyes. He stuck his head inside Daniel's locker to push some books to the back of the shelf, then held out his left hand. "Hand me some balloons," he said, his voice muffled.

It seemed to Dee that he was trying to hide from her, but she couldn't imagine why. She grabbed a red balloon from the bag and placed it in his hand. The balloon quickly disappeared into the locker, and then Ted's hand stretched back again for reloading.

Fitting a blue balloon into his hand this time, she said, "You know, we could do this a lot faster if you'd get out of the locker so we could both stuff it."

He backed out, a faint blush on his cheeks. "You're right. But I bet I can get more in than you."

Dee or Denise, there was no way she could ignore such a challenge. She pushed the lawn bag between them, and they went to work. Twice their arms got tangled together as they dipped deep into the bag. Both times Dee looked up in surprise and saw something new on Ted's face.

Less than five minutes later the locker was almost full. Only one balloon was left, and Denise handed it to Ted. He tucked it into a space below the shelf, but it somehow disturbed the delicate balance inside the locker. Balloons rubbed against one another, and four of them popped loose to float into the hall.

"Get them," Ted told her.

"Why me?" Denise asked, laughing. For a minute he'd sounded just like Daniel. But she knew Ted wasn't really trying to push her around.

"Because you're shorter."

"What does that have to do with anything?"

"You can't do this," Ted explained and flattened himself against the open locker. Dee saw at once that with his long legs together and his arms pressed inward to fill the small gaps on each side of him, Ted was making sure no more balloons could escape.

Quickly she ran after the four runaways and dropped them back into the bag. Then, while Ted held back the flow, she tucked one balloon into the locker on either side of his head. They fit snugly, so snugly that it looked as if the last two would have to be pushed in around his waist. Dee started to nudge a yellow one past him, but when her arm touched his belt, she jumped back as if she'd been given an electric shock.

"Maybe you should do the last two," she said. She could feel her face getting warm.

"Embarrassed?"

"Me? No. I just want to be fair. I did two of them, and you should do the others," she babbled.

"You're not counting them *again?*" he said, pretending to be shocked. "We already counted them the first time they went into the locker."

"If we both put two in, it won't matter," she said, and handed him the yellow balloon.

Carefully he shifted his body first to one side and then the other, pushing the balloons in behind him. "Now comes the hard part. We have to get the door shut."

"I've got an idea. I could just close you inside with all the balloons. That would really surprise Daniel."

"Funny, Denise," he grumbled. "But seriously, start closing it slowly. I'll jump out at the last minute."

"Keep your fingers out of the way," she warned, and inched the metal door toward Ted. Just as he'd promised, he jumped out at the right time. No balloons escaped, and no part of Ted remained inside the locker.

"We're not done yet," Ted told her, reaching into his gym bag. He pulled out a roll of crepe paper and handed it to her.

She took the white roll and started to unwind it. Pink letters danced across the paper, spelling out "Happy Birthday—Happy Birthday—Happy Birthday."

"What do you think?" Ted asked. He was watching her, waiting anxiously for her reaction.

"I love it. Daniel is going to die!"

"I really thought you'd like it. I bought it for you."

"Really?" Dee looked at Ted, suddenly curious. She was sure he knew the pink birthday wishes would embarrass Daniel. So there was no other way to explain it—he really *had* bought the crepe paper for her. He knew how much she wanted to pay her brother back for all the tricks he'd played on her. "Thanks," she said and smiled at him.

Working quickly, she draped the crepe paper across the locker door, then taped it at the top corners so it drooped in the center. Long pieces hung down on each side. Stepping back, she put her hands on her hips to admire her work.

"And that's not all." Ted's hand disappeared into his gym bag again and came out with an envelope. He handed it to Dee.

She lifted the flap and pulled out a baby photograph. "This is Daniel's baby picture."

"Yeah," he said, a look of triumph in his eyes.

"How'd you get it?"

"Your mom gave it to me," he said, holding the tape while she centered the photograph on the locker door.

"You're kidding!" Dee couldn't believe it. Even her mom had been in on the trick to give Daniel a taste of his own medicine. Kids were starting to walk down the halls and laughed as Dee held the picture against the locker door and Ted taped it down. Daniel was going to wish he'd never gotten out of bed.

"I think it's done," Ted told her, stowing the supplies in his gym bag. "Want to get some juice from the machine in the cafeteria?"

"Great idea." She grabbed her backpack by its straps. "Could we stop by the bulletin board in the lobby? The callback sheets for *Oklahoma!* are supposed to be posted by now."

"Sure. But don't forget your bag."

The empty lawn bag was lying in a heap on the floor. Ted picked it up and stuffed it into her pack while she held it open.

They didn't talk on the way to the bulletin board; Dee was too nervous. She wanted a part in the play so much. What if her name wasn't on the list?

There was a crowd around the board, and Denise was too short to see over all the heads. "Ted, I'll never be able to see if my name is up there."

He grabbed her hand and started moving into the crowd. "Come with me," he called over his shoulder.

She scurried to catch up with him. Ted didn't seem to be pushing his way through the group, he was just finding the gaps between bodies and slipping through them. When they reached the bulletin board, he pulled her next to him.

"There it is," he said happily and pointed to the fifth name from the top. "Denise Davidson."

"Denise Davidson," she whispered. "I did it!" She realized they were still holding hands when she crushed his in her excitement. He squeezed back.

"Let's get some juice to celebrate. My treat."

"OK," she said. She could not seem to stop smiling. The next day she would be on the stage again, auditioning as Ado Annie.

They plopped into side-by-side seats in the cafeteria. Ted was sipping his juice through a straw when suddenly he started to smile.

"What's so funny?" Dee asked.

"I was remembering how you looked with that sack of balloons over your shoulder. You looked like a short, skinny Santa Claus." He started to laugh.

Dee looked down at her outfit and had to admit he was right. The red-striped sweater and red pants *did* fit the image. She began to laugh with him.

Finally he regained control of his voice. "I knew you hadn't forgotten how to have fun. Your eyes still sparkle, even if you don't want them to. You haven't killed off Dee completely."

She stopped smiling. If he was right, she told herself, she'd have to be really careful. "Ted, please don't tell anyone about this morning."

"Why shouldn't I talk about it? We didn't do anything wrong."

"I know, but Jeremy might not understand." A knot was beginning to twist and tighten in her stomach.

"I'm sure not going to tell *him*."

"But if you tell anyone, it might get back to him. He likes the new me. We've got a date Friday night, and I don't want anything to spoil it. Will you promise?"

His hands circled the juice can, ready to crush it. "OK. I won't say anything about this morning," he agreed, his voice rough. "I don't know why you want to date someone who doesn't like you the way you really are."

"How can you be so sure Denise isn't the real me?" she asked defensively, surprised at how bad it made her feel to think he didn't like the new Denise.

"I know Dee is the real you because this new person can't even have a good time with her friends anymore. Can you live the rest of your life without playing another practical joke or laughing so hard that you finally cry?"

"Of course not," she said defensively. "But I won't have to."

"I know what kind of guy Jeremy Griffin is, and I wouldn't be so sure of that." The juice can collapsed with a crunch.

Chapter Six

"I hear her upstairs. You're going to see my sister in her biggest role ever," Daniel called out from the living room couch where he was lounging.

"What part is that?" Ted asked. He was sprawled out in a chair on the opposite side of the room.

"Jeremy Griffin's date. Hey, Denise, I've heard that if you're good enough at this Deborah act, it could get you an Oscar nomination."

"Yeah?" she answered, still out of sight on the landing. "Well, Johnny Carson might be interested in your imitation of a couch potato." Dee didn't want to be trading insults with her brother when Jeremy was due any minute, but there was no way she was going to let his teasing pass unanswered.

She knew his comment about her "biggest role" had nothing to do with the part of Ado

Annie she'd gotten in the school play. It was about her date with Jeremy. Most of his mean jokes the last few days involved her date with Jeremy. He hadn't stopped insulting her since he'd found his locker decorated on Tuesday.

Ignoring Ted and her brother, she arranged the gathers in her full skirt and started to walk down the stairs. She figured Jeremy would prefer it if she wore a dress, but she didn't own one. Actually, she'd been desperate enough to try on Deborah's dresses, but they'd made her feel as if Deborah would be going out with Jeremy instead of Denise—and that would have ruined the whole thing. Getting a date with one of the Griffin brothers was Denise's triumph—not Deborah's.

So she had chosen a wool challis print skirt covered with pink rosebuds and green vines. The full panels fell in graceful folds. She wore a green sweater with a scooped neck and black low-heeled boots to complete the outfit.

The hardest thing had been getting her hair to behave. She'd slicked the sides back with gel but the waves hadn't been too excited about staying flat. When she had finally threatened to cut them off, they agreed to cooperate. Then she had fluffed the top and angled the bangs across her forehead, adding pink earrings to match the flowers in her skirt as the finishing touch. Dee knew she looked different than ever before, and she knew she looked good.

She walked across the living room and peered out the front window. The driveway was empty, and the street was quiet. Sighing, Dee dropped into a chair next to Ted. She'd just have to suffer her brother's insults a little longer.

"What have you done with my sister?" Daniel demanded. "How am I going to explain to Jeremy that *you* came downstairs instead of Dee or Denise?"

"If that's a compliment, thank you," Denise said sweetly.

She turned to Ted, expecting him to say something about her appearance, too. But he just stared at her. She blinked and checked again. He looked as if he were in shock or something. Well, at least she wouldn't have to listen to another lecture from him.

"I don't know which is more weird—" Daniel declared from his lounging position.

Dee didn't bother to ask him what he meant. She could count on her brother to finish the statement with another sarcastic remark.

"Which will be stranger?" he continued. "Your date with Jeremy? Or Allison's blind date with the captain of the football team?"

Dee frowned. Her head had been so full of thoughts about her own date that she'd completely forgotten her best friend was going out that night, too. A friend of Allison's older brother had set up the date. Everyone knew the football captain had the social skills of a bear.

Now, instead of answering Daniel, Dee shrugged and peered out the window again. Allison might have an unusual evening ahead, but she didn't appreciate her brother comparing it to her own date. As she turned, she noticed that Ted was still watching her.

"There's one good thing about this date," her brother said. "If you play it just right, you could find out how he got that picture of the president for his locker."

Denise had to laugh when he said that. Allison had been nagging her to ask Jeremy the same question. Everyone wanted to know about Jeremy's picture of himself with the president. Denise hadn't even seen it yet.

"If I get a chance, I'll ask just for you."

"How about that, Ted? We'll be among the first to know," Daniel said, joking.

Denise didn't hear Ted's reply because at that moment a car pulled into the driveway. It had to be Jeremy! The big date was finally happening! Wiping her suddenly damp palms on her skirt, she tried to control her pounding heart. If Denise didn't stay in control, Dee would ruin the evening.

Slowly she walked to the door. Dee thought she heard footsteps on the sidewalk but made herself stand still, hands at her sides, until he rang the doorbell. It chimed once, and she decided to wait for him to ring a second time.

"Can't you answer the door?" Daniel hooted. "You're standing right next to it."

Deborah had never run to the door on the first ring. It would have made her dates think she was anxious to greet them. After the doorbell tolled again, Denise opened the door and greeted Jeremy with a smile.

"Good evening," he said, his voice strong and masculine. Denise felt her knees turning to jelly when he stepped inside. He stood so close to her that she could smell his musky cologne. He peeked into the living room. "Aren't your parents here?"

"No," she managed to whisper. She handed him her coat and he held it while she slipped into it. "They went out to dinner."

"I'm here," Daniel announced, finally getting off the couch. He stretched his legs and started to cross the room. "Hi, Jeremy, Denise has to be home by ten o'clock."

Jeremy looked at Daniel and then at Dee.

She took his arm and moved closer to him. "Don't listen to him. Let's get out of here."

With a quick goodbye for Daniel and Ted,

Jeremy nudged Dee toward the door. She glanced over her shoulder, giving her brother a withering look. Daniel shrugged, but it was Ted who caught her eye. His lips were set in a tight line, and he looked disappointed. His reaction was strange, but she decided she wasn't going to think about him that night. It was time to start enjoying her triumph—the best date of her life.

They stepped into the brisk night air, and Jeremy pulled her against his side. "What movie would you like to see?"

"*Princess Sara*," she replied. It was the hottest romantic comedy of the season.

"Really?" He sounded disappointed. "I was thinking of taking you to *The Last Volcano*."

Even the advertising for that movie had made Denise imagine things were crawling on her back all night. "There are snakes in it," she said, her husky voice crackling.

"You don't want to see that movie?"

Denise just looked at him—and thought about snakes.

"Let's go see *Princess Sara*," he said.

He made small talk on the way to the theater while Dee tilted her seat back and tried to relax. He was driving a Thunderbird, which she assumed belonged to his father. She'd never really thought about it, but somehow it seemed fitting that Jeremy would drive an American-made car. He was so—well, so all-American.

Jeremy bought their tickets and headed straight for the theater doors, not even looking back to see if Dee was following him. Surprised, she stopped in the middle of the lobby. She was willing to give up a lot of things to date Jeremy Griffin, but popcorn at the movies was not one of them. Stubbornly she marched to the concession stand.

When Jeremy discovered she was no longer at his side, he turned around to look for her. "Did you want something?" he called out when he spotted her.

"Please," she said, complimenting herself for being so polite. "Buttered popcorn," she instructed the boy behind the counter as Jeremy joined her.

Jeremy slid two dollars toward the register. Drumming his fingers on the counter, he watched her cradle the tub lovingly in her arms. "Aren't you going to get napkins?"

Napkins? Dee never needed napkins with her popcorn. She and Allison usually licked their fingers in the dark once the movie started. Still—this was Jeremy. And he was with Denise. "Sure. I forgot. Could you grab a few?"

Dating Jeremy was certainly going to be a challenge. Dee had thought the hard part would be getting him to ask her out, but staying on her best behavior during the date was going to be tricky, too. But she felt confident she could handle it—and even have a good time.

The movie opened with the princess character tripping out of a cab and landing in a puddle at the hero's feet. Dee, or at least the remains of Dee, could relate to that disaster. It was funny, so she started to laugh.

As usual, the honking-geese sound of her laughter attracted attention. Even in the dark, she could sense heads turning. Apparently Jeremy felt it, too.

"Do you have to do that?" he asked, trying to make it sound like a casual question.

She squinted at him and saw that he was actually upset. His mouth was set in a tight, grim line, and his eyes—his eyes had turned cold.

"No, I don't need to laugh," she muttered.

The bright lights at the Burger Den were a shock after the movie theater and the drive to the restaurant. Denise blinked in surprise.

"Feel like a mole coming up for air?" Jeremy asked, teasing.

She tried to grin, but her face hurt too much from smiling. Since she hadn't been able to laugh during the movie, she'd forced herself to smile instead. And the funnier the movie got, the harder she'd smiled. Now her face felt as if it had been frozen in a smile for days.

They ordered hamburgers and fries. It was quiet at their table, and Denise knew someone had better start a conversation—soon.

"How'd you like the movie?" she asked cheerfully. "I thought it was great."

"It was—different."

"You didn't like it. I'm sorry."

"I didn't say it was bad," he said quickly.

Always so polite, Dee thought. *So polite he can't even admit he hated the movie!* "Never mind," she said kindly. "I appreciate your taking me." Silence again. Dee shifted nervously in her seat. There had to be something else they could discuss. She searched her brain until she found a topic. "Why don't you tell me more about your band tour?"

Deborah had always recommended asking boys to talk about themselves. And now Dee learned her sister had been right. Jeremy listed the songs they would play, the sights they would see, the cities they would pass on their bus trip. The food was delivered, and Denise had finished half her hamburger before he came up for air.

"Ketchup?" She handed him the bottle as she tried to think of something else to ask about the trip. He didn't seem to have left anything out, but she wanted him to think she was really interested. "Do you carry your instruments with you?"

"No. We'll have an extra bus just for the instruments. This is a first-class trip."

Obviously, she realized. Now she was completely out of conversation ideas.

"What about you?" Jeremy asked. "Did you get a part in the play?"

The cast had been announced that morning, and since she hadn't seen him during the day at school, she hadn't had a chance to share her news with him. But how was she going to tell him she'd gotten the part she really wanted? He thought her heart was set on Laurie, the lead.

"I got a pretty big part," she said and bent forward to study a french fry.

"Not the lead?" he questioned.

"No. Some senior will be playing Laurie. I'm going to be Ado Annie." She held her breath and slowly looked up to see the expression on his face. Ado Annie was a funny character. Was he going to think she was reverting back to Dee?

His eyes were sparkling, and he looked amused. "So you're going to be 'the girl who can't say no,' " he said, grinning.

"Yeah." She nodded, thinking she should have known he would associate the part with the character's most famous line.

"This should make you an interesting girl to have around."

Although every muscle in her face ached, she smiled. It was the closest thing to a joke that Jeremy had made yet.

Laughter drifted to them from across the room. Dee turned and spied some of her friends. They were sharing three baskets of onion rings and laughing themselves silly. She didn't understand what was so funny. Her friends weren't looking in her direction, so she knew they couldn't be joking about her. Dee glanced in the direction they were in and spotted Allison in the corner with her football player.

The guy seemed to know everyone in the restaurant. An endless stream of people stopped at their table, mostly his teammates. Through it all, Allison was tapping her long nails on the tabletop.

Every time someone new started monopolizing her date, Allison would turn to her group of friends, roll her eyes and shake her head. Her gaudy earrings sparkled off the overhead lights, but they were not as bright as her dancing eyes. Allison was handling her date and his fans with her usual sense of humor.

It was easy for Dee to imagine the conversation at her friends' table. They would be making jokes about the guy and inventing lines Allison should be using on him. A few phrases drifted toward her.

"He is *so* dumb."

"How dumb is he?"

"So dumb he can't remember Allison is his date!"

They hooted, and Allison grinned when she heard them.

Suddenly Dee felt left out. She should be over there with her group. But she was too busy being Denise, too busy trying to impress Jeremy. She didn't like it, being left out.

"Is something wrong?"

Dee whipped back around to face Jeremy. "Why do you ask?"

"You've been staring across the room with an unhappy look on your face," Jeremy explained.

"Unhappy? When I'm with you?" she asked. That was one of Deborah's lines. Her sister believed in flattering men to get out of awkward situations. And it worked: Jeremy smiled at her and relaxed.

Dee was relieved when they left Burger Den before anything else could happen. She had been half-afraid her friends would stop by the table to tease her.

The drive home was quiet, and Dee used the time to think. Her Jeremy Griffin date hadn't been the earthshaking event of her dreams, but she told herself she'd probably expected too much. He was a nice guy, and they had shared a pretty good time.

They were almost to her house when she remembered Daniel's question. She stared at the lights on the car radio. "Could I ask you something kind of personal?"

He looked over for two seconds, and she knew she'd gotten his attention. "Let's hear the question."

"Do you really have a picture in your locker of yourself with the president of the United States?"

"I do."

A car was approaching from the other lane, and the headlights helped her see his smile. "How did you get it?" she asked.

"That makes two questions."

She wished he hadn't said that. It made him sound like her brother. "But they go together."

"OK," he agreed. "My dad worked on the campaign for one of our U.S. senators. When our family took a trip to Washington, D.C., Senator Thomas arranged for us to meet the president."

"Your dad must be quite a campaigner," she said, slightly awed. Her mom had helped a neighbor get elected to the city school board, but that hadn't done a thing for Dee's relationship with Hill High's principal. Mr. Griffin must be pretty important.

"He was in charge of Thomas's campaign," Jeremy explained, trying to sound modest. "Would you like to see the picture?"

"Yes."

"Why don't you meet me at my locker Monday morning? Do you know where it is?"

"Yeah." His head turned sharply in surprise, and Dee knew she'd just put her foot in her mouth. Now he knew she had scouted out his locker.

Jeremy pulled the car to the curb in front of Dee's house. She waited in her seat while he walked around the car and opened her door. Real star treatment. He reached for her hand, and they strolled toward her door.

"I had a nice time tonight," he said softly.

"You did?" She knew Deborah expected her dates to have a good time, but Dee wasn't that sure of herself.

"Yes, I did. Are you surprised?"

She had embarrassed him by laughing during the movie. Then she'd ignored him and watched her friends at the Burger Den. Mary Beth Kramer didn't have a laugh that attracted male geese. Mary Beth Kramer would never be rude and ignore the person she was out with. Mary Beth Kramer might be boring and predictable, but Dee thought Jeremy would probably have had a better time with her.

Deborah had once told her that some questions were better left unanswered. Dee decided Jeremy's was one of them. "I had a nice time, too," she said simply.

They were still holding hands as they walked up the steps to her door. He tugged on her right hand until she turned to face him. Dee thought he might be planning to kiss her, but then she decided it was too much to hope for this soon.

"Will you meet me for lunch on Monday?" he asked softly.

"Yes," she whispered.

"And Tuesday?"

"No problem."

His hands gently gripped her shoulders and he pulled her closer to him. He leaned toward her, and suddenly Denise knew it *was* going to happen!

It was a quick kiss. He pressed his lips against hers for a few seconds and then moved away with a smile. "Good night."

"Good night," she said weakly as he backed down the steps.

Denise had never actually kissed a fish, but something told her it would feel exactly like kissing Jeremy. *So he isn't perfect after all*, she thought. She had to stifle a giggle for fear he might hear it.

The door whipped open. "Get inside," Daniel hissed.

As she stepped into the house, Dee wiped her hand over her lips.

"Don't bother trying to hide it. I saw him kiss you," Daniel taunted.

"And that's not all—" she replied smugly. Daniel raised his eyebrows, and in the living room she saw Ted get up from his chair. For a moment Dee wondered if he'd sat in the same spot all night watching TV.

"What else happened?" Ted asked in a gruff voice.

"I found out how he got that picture of the president!"

Daniel tried to punch her, but she ducked. She heard Ted heave a sigh of relief. Curiously, she wondered what they had expected her to say.

After telling them about the picture, she bid the boys good night and climbed the stairs to her room. It had been a long night and she was exhausted. Still, the adrenaline pumping through her veins—the result of having accomplished the most important goal she'd ever set for herself—promised it would be hours before she fell asleep. She lay back on her bed, dropped her shoes on the floor, and resorted to one of

Dee's favorite moves. She kicked her feet in the air and giggled. Then her gaze strayed to the valentine on her dresser.

"He might not be as romantic as my mystery admirer, but I did it! I really did it! I had a date with Jeremy Griffin!"

Chapter Seven

"How are we going to find out which states observe Columbus Day as a holiday?" Allison asked as she crushed her scavenger hunt assignment sheet in her hand.

"I've got a better question," Dee said, gloomily scanning the shelves of reference books in the library. Their study period was nearly over, and so far they'd only been able to answer four questions. "Why did we wait until the last minute to start this project? We've had over two weeks to do this work."

She felt a hand on her shoulder and knew immediately who was behind her. Jeremy. He'd become her shadow since their first date eleven days before.

"I didn't see you at lunch today," he whispered in her ear.

She looked up and saw a mixture of disappointment and surprise on his face. He obviously wasn't used to dating a girl whose life didn't revolve around him. "I had to meet with the cast. We're planning our rehearsal schedule for next week's vacation."

"I'm going to miss you while I'm in Florida."

"I'll miss you, too," she said quickly.

"Since the band is leaving Friday afternoon right after school, could we have dinner Thursday night?"

Dee thought for a minute. All of her assignments would be done by then, and she couldn't think of anything else she needed to do Thursday night. "That'd be fine."

"Good. I'll make a reservation at Mama Gabby's." He patted her on the shoulder. "I've got some studying to do, I'll see you later."

Dee offered a weak wave in his direction. Mama Gabby's meant Italian food and, more specifically, spaghetti. She had two days to practice twirling pasta on her fork. Jeremy certainly wouldn't appreciate it if she sucked the long noodles into her mouth—the way she did at home to annoy Daniel.

But right then she had to worry about finishing her English assignment. She'd think about Thursday night later. Turning back to her scavenger hunt notes, she tried to make a deal with Allison. "If you'll take the holiday question, I'll try to find out how tall Winston Churchill was."

"Wait a minute." Allison grabbed Dee's sleeve before she could escape. "What's going on between you and Jeremy?"

Dee squinted at her friend, wondering what had prompted her question. "We're dating, you know that."

"At least he's acting that way. I'd say you're not very friendly with him, considering how long you chased the guy."

Dee looked down at her notes to avoid facing her friend. Allison was right. Jeremy had decided the new Denise was the girl for him, and he was leaving her very little time for herself. He called her every night. He expected her to meet him at his locker before and after school. She had been his lunch companion each noon since their first date.

She imagined she could enjoy him a little more if she wasn't always working so hard to maintain her Denise personality. Twice she'd awakened from nightmares in which she'd switched back to Dee in front of Jeremy.

"You're too quiet," Allison said, breaking into Dee's thoughts. "Something's wrong."

The librarian glared at them, and the two girls retreated to the magazine reading area. They sat on an empty couch.

"You're not exactly wrong," Dee confessed.

"This relationship isn't working out the way I expected."

"And I can guess *who* the problem is."

Dee's head jerked up. Did Allison know how tired she was of acting all the time?

"Jeremy's the problem," concluded her friend. "He's no fun. I bet you're bored to death. Why can't you just admit dating him is a mistake?"

"Because it's not!" The librarian turned at Dee's outburst. "It's not a mistake," she repeated softly. She buried her face in a newspaper, trying to shut out Allison's doubtful expression.

How could it be a mistake? Dee asked herself. She had the one thing that Deborah had never been able to get—a Griffin. And there was something else, too: something that had nothing to do with beating Deborah. Dee felt more confident now that she'd proved to her brother and everyone else that she was more than just a clown. She had learned that she didn't have to make people laugh in order to get along with them.

There were times she missed the old Dee. The week before she had nearly left the house with her T-shirt on inside out. She had hurried back up to her room to fix it, remembering she never used to check the hall mirror before leaving the house. Before Jeremy, she would have gone to school with seams and tags flapping in the wind.

Not being the center of attention had advantages. She felt a kind of freedom now that her classmates didn't expect her to put on a show at least once a day. Her grades were improving because she listened to her teachers more often during class.

Allison kicked Dee to get her attention. "What's that?"

"It sounds like singing." Dee cocked her head, listening.

"*Bad* singing," Allison corrected. "It's coming from one of the listening rooms."

Allison jumped up to look for the "singer," and Dee followed slowly.

"Hey! It's Jeremy's blond friend." Allison seemed delighted to have found Alex making a fool of himself.

Dee had to smile at the sight. Alex was playing a tape and listening through the headphones. He was singing along with the music, and he obviously didn't realize his voice was carrying.

When he reached for a high note, both girls cringed. "What should we do?" Allison asked, a mischievous grin on her face.

"Nothing."

"You're just saying that because he's Jeremy's friend," she complained.

"Not really. Think how embarrassed anyone would be if they were caught doing that," Dee pointed out.

"It didn't bother you," Allison countered.

That wasn't exactly true. When Dee's friends had teased her for doing the same thing in the fall, she wanted to crawl under the table. Some of them had pounded on the window, and others had covered their ears as if she were painfully off-key. But *Dee* hadn't let them see her embarrassment. She had simply opened the door and told her friends to "hold their applause and just throw money."

She knew Alex didn't have enough of a sense of humor to help him deal with the kind of joke Allison had in mind. Like Jeremy, he took himself too seriously. Dee also knew he didn't especially like her; he'd never forgive her if she helped Allison.

"Look, do whatever you want, but I can't be part of it," she said, and started to walk away.

"Denise Davidson," Allison hissed in frustration. "Jeremy Griffin has turned you into a total bore. Why did you have to kill off *Dee* and start going with him?" Her friend spun around and bounced out of the library.

Just then Dee felt the ever-familiar tap on her shoulder. "Is something the matter?" Jeremy asked.

"You might want to step around the corner and tell Alex he's been serenading us," she said, trying to calm down. Allison's words had hurt her a lot.

Jeremy disappeared into the listening room, and Dee gathered up her papers. One more study period had passed, and she still hadn't completed the scavenger hunt. Now she would have to stay after school to finish it before Thursday. She looked up as Alex came out of the room and quickly left the library, then smiled at Jeremy as he rejoined her.

"Thanks for telling me," he said. "It would have been embarrassing for Alex if someone else had gone in there."

"That's what I thought." She felt a little better, knowing that Jeremy agreed with her. She hadn't meant to offend Allison, but she'd realized that Alex had feelings, too.

"I'll walk you to your last class," Jeremy offered.

"I'd like that."

They stepped into the hall and Jeremy stopped at the drinking fountain. As he started to straighten up, he paused to stare at Dee's legs.

"There's something hanging from your pants," he explained, reaching over to tug at her hem. Other people in the hall slowed down to watch.

She felt him pull something from the inside of her pant leg, and she couldn't imagine what he'd found. People giggled, and when he placed a dryer sheet across her books, she wanted to hide inside the closest locker. Why hadn't she seen it in the mirror before she left for school? Why couldn't Allison have been the one to find it? Why did these things always have to happen to her?

"What is it?" he asked.

One look at his genuinely curious eyes told Dee he really didn't know. "It's a dryer sheet."

"A what?"

Didn't he ever help with the laundry? she wondered. Probably not. Daniel acted as if his hands would fall off if they touched detergent or bleach. She tried to explain the function of the white sheet draped across her books. "It's something you put into the dryer to soften your clothes and take the static out."

"Doesn't it dissolve or something?"

"Obviously not," she muttered.

His innocence was almost cute, but his questions were making her uncomfortable. *Dee* would have had this matter settled by now. She would have wadded up the sheet and tossed it into the nearest wastebasket as if it were a basketball. Then she'd have called out, "Two points," and the whole incident would have been forgotten. But it wasn't that easy for *Denise*. She was going to have to talk her way out of this awkward spot.

"You're supposed to remove the little sheet from the dry clothes, but sometimes you can't find it," she told him.

"Where does it go?"

"Inside pant legs—up sleeves—wherever it sticks." She smiled and nonchalantly tucked the sheet inside her notebook. Inside, she was cringing. Embarrassing situations were hard for Denise, she thought.

"Amazing," he concluded with a nod. "I'll have to tell my mom about them."

Jeremy ordered spaghetti and meatballs for both of them and then leaned back in his chair. He reached out for the candle in the center of the table, tipping its glass bowl at an angle, and watching as the flame flickered as the melted wax nearly extinguished the fire.

"I'm really going to miss you, Denise," he said sincerely.

"Of course, and I'll miss you, too." Dee knew she didn't sound as convincing as he had.

"You've been a surprise," he said, tilting his head to one side as if studying her. "Who would have guessed a month ago that I would be dating Denise Davidson?"

"Me," she told him with a smile.

"That's right." He threw back his head and laughed. "I wouldn't have looked at you twice if you hadn't rushed up to me with your Cupid's Arrow survey." He squared his shoulders proudly. "It felt pretty good being pursued."

He had *liked* the idea of her chasing him? If he was telling her the truth, she could have been more obvious about her plan and gotten his attention before Christmas. The time she'd sprained her ankle trying to spy on him—that would have been a perfect setup. She could have cried out for help, and he would have discovered her and been impressed by the steps she was taking to pursue him. Instead, she'd limped away in silence.

"You were pretty cute Valentine's Day." Her head popped up in surprise. "When you looked up at me with those big eyes, I could see how badly you wanted me to ask you out."

Dee was beginning to get irritated. It was nice to hear he liked her eyes, but cocker spaniels had big eyes, too. And it made her feel pretty stupid to learn he liked them because they made him feel more important.

The waitress arrived with a basket of garlic toast. The smell made Dee's mouth water, and she reached for a piece. But just as she had chosen the one she wanted, the basket moved. Her hand followed the bread, but Jeremy kept sliding it away from her.

"Do you really want to have *garlic breath*?" he whispered.

"Why not?" She couldn't imagine letting the delicious toast just sit there. Uneaten. "If we both have it, it won't make any difference."

He nodded and set the basket between them. They ate for a few minutes. When Jeremy finished his piece of toast, he used a napkin to pat the crumbs off his lips. "Will you be rehearsing while I'm on tour?"

Before answering, she licked the last morsels of bread from her lips. She felt a stubborn crumb sticking to the corner of her mouth, and stretched her tongue out to catch it. Jeremy gritted his teeth in disgust. Deciding to ignore the look on his face, Dee simply answered the question. "The cast is getting together twice. We have to be ready for our first rehearsal with the orchestra."

"That'll be fun. My band friends will be surprised when they hear how well you sing—even if you don't have the lead."

"I think it'll be fun playing Ado Annie," she said cautiously. It was the first time Jeremy had heard her admit her real feelings about the part.

His eyebrows arched, but all he said was, "If you say so."

The spaghetti arrived, and Denise watched Jeremy twirl the noodles around his fork with an easy twist of the wrist. How did he do that? she wondered. Last night she'd discovered an old box of noodles in the cupboard and had boiled them to practice with. Every time she'd turned the fork, half of the noodles had unwound themselves and fallen back toward the plate. She'd decided it was hopeless.

Trying now to be inconspicuous, Dee used her fork to cut the pasta into manageable chunks.

"That's cute," Jeremy said, sounding more like a sophisticated uncle than her date.

"It's better than doing this." She found a long noodle and sucked it slowly into her mouth, watching his astonished expression the whole time. She knew Dee had escaped for a minute, but she didn't mind. It was worth it to see his mouth hanging open. He obviously didn't realize how silly it made him look. She dabbed her chin with a napkin and challenged him with a wide grin.

"Yes. Cutting the noodles is a much better idea." He shook his head. "You're certainly an interesting person."

The evening was definitely turning weird. Dee was getting the idea that Jeremy wasn't too sure why he liked her. She was clearly different from any other girls he had dated. Apparently they

didn't have problems with dryer sheets or spaghetti, and they didn't aspire to play Ado Annie.
They must be a pretty dull group of girls, Dee
decided.

Jeremy suggested a walk after dinner. The restaurant was in a mall, so they decided to
window-shop.

"Look at that," Dee said. The mannequin was
wearing a sunshine yellow outfit—cotton pants
and a striped shirt. She knew it would look perfect on her.

"That makes me think of spring, and you."

"How poetic," she said softly, touched by his
thoughtful comment.

His arm stretched behind her back, and he
rested a hand on her shoulder. "I don't think you
know how impressed I am by your new image."

Dee couldn't help grinning. It had been hard
work to be thinking constantly about changing
her looks and watching her behavior. But she
liked it when someone appreciated what she was
trying to do. The only person who had said anything about her new image, aside from Allison,
had been Daniel—and he had insulted her.

"*Everyone* has noticed the new Denise
Davidson. And they've noticed that I'm dating
the new Denise," he explained smugly. "Just
think how much that's going to help me when I

run for senior class president next year. No one is going to say 'Jeremy who?' "

"I suppose not," she mumbled, her thoughts spinning so fast she couldn't sort them out.

Jeremy had mentioned several things he liked about her—but each one, it seemed, benefited him. Being chased had fed his ego. Her beautiful brown eyes had made him feel powerful. He wanted her to do well in *Oklahoma!* because he would be showing her off to his buddies. And he was planning to use her reputation to help him win the election next fall. Dee's eyes narrowed. Maybe he thought the world revolved around Jeremy Griffin, but she didn't agree.

She thought about being his girlfriend until the elections, and the idea made her feel sick. Could she survive six more months of blow drying her hair every morning? Her brain might fry. Could she keep up her new image during the summer? June and July were Dee's favorite months. Just the thought of going to the beach with Jeremy and maintaining Denise's good behavior was exhausting.

Jeremy assumed they would still be together in September. Dee knew some changes would have to be made before that happened, and this time she wasn't going to be the one to make concessions.

On the way home Jeremy talked about the

band trip and reminded her once again how much he would miss her. Dee wanted him to be quiet. It had been a strange evening, and she needed time to think about the things he had said.

"You don't have to walk me to the door," she said quickly as he pulled up to the curb. "I'm sure you need to pack tonight, and it's getting late."

"I've been packed for two days." He hopped out of the car and walked around to her door. He helped her out, and his arm circled her waist, holding her close as they moved toward the house. When she reached for the doorknob, he stopped her. "Don't go in yet."

Dee turned to face him, and he slipped a hand under her chin. He tilted her head back and gazed at her as if memorizing her face for those lonely days and nights in Florida. She knew he was going to kiss her, but what was taking him so long? She wanted to be done with it.

He kept staring, so she decided to take the matter into her own hands. Quickly, she stretched up and placed a kiss on his lips. "Have a good trip, Jeremy," she said softly and disappeared into the house.

Daniel jumped off the couch. "Have a *good* date?"

"Stuff it," she muttered, heading for the stairs.

"Feeling sad that he's leaving you?" he called to her back.

She wished she could feel sad, she admitted as she closed her bedroom door and leaned against it. Sad would be better than what she was feeling. Realizing she had wasted most of her year chasing Jeremy made her feel awful. She *had* managed to date a Griffin, something she could flaunt in Deborah's face when her sister came home the next week, but that was about the only good thing she could say about Jeremy Griffin at the moment.

Allison was right: he was boring. And he was also the most self-centered person she had ever met. If she was lucky, his band would tour Epcot Center, and Jeremy would get lost—permanently lost.

Chapter Eight

"If you're not going outside, close the door," Deborah called from the kitchen table.

Dee held the door open with a foot and leaned on the frame. She could smell dinner cooking in the house as she watched her brother and Ted tossing a baseball around the backyard. Although the sky was cloudy and the weatherman had predicted snow, it was a fairly warm afternoon—by March standards. The ground was starting to thaw, and the guys were sinking into the soft earth as they chased the ball.

"I'm cold," Deborah complained.

"Close the door," Dee's mother said firmly.

"Fine," she mumbled, slipping outside and perching on the top step. Why had Deborah come home during break? she wondered gloomily. Other college kids went to Florida, but, no—Deborah had to come home. Probably just to ruin my vacation, Dee thought.

111

Daniel had made the "Jeremy announcement" before she'd had a chance to do it herself. During Sunday dinner he had looked across the table at Deborah and said, "Denise is dating Jeremy Griffin," in one of his more annoying tones.

"So?" Deborah hadn't even bothered to look at him.

"He's one of 'those Griffins'—the ones you couldn't get a date with if your life depended on it."

Dee had almost liked her brother at that second. After her disastrous dinner with Jeremy, she'd decided she didn't want to date him again; but she wouldn't admit that until her sister had been duly impressed by her accomplishment. And if Dee and Daniel agreed on anything, it was their mutual desire to see Deborah squirm.

"Is that right?" their sister asked and yawned. Then she glanced at Dee as if wondering how her little sister had gotten anyone to date her.

"It sure is," Dee replied, ready to savor her victory. "He'd be over here today, except that he's in Florida on a band tour."

"That's nice," Deborah said, dishing more salad onto her plate. "Mom, have I told you about Ben Richards? He's the one whose father owns some football team."

And that had been the end of the Griffin discussion. The end of Dee's imagined victory.

She had waited and plotted for a whole year to get a date with Jeremy. She'd stifled her laughter and offended her friends in order to be Jeremy's girl. And why had she done it? To impress Deborah. To make Deborah notice her. To prove to Deborah that she was a woman, too.

And Deborah doesn't care! she reminded herself, kicking a loose stone on the cement steps.

"Dinner is about ready," her mother called through a crack in the door. "Would you help, please?"

Dee laughed at Daniel when Ted's pitch whizzed past his ear, and then reluctantly she went inside. Daniel and Ted tramped into the house. Deborah was tossing a salad. Dee was setting the table. Mr. Davidson was slicing the ham, and Mrs. Davidson was dishing the vegetables.

The guys stamped their feet. "It's starting to snow. Can Ted stay for dinner?" Daniel asked from across the room.

Mrs. Davidson looked around at the busy workers. "What harm could one more cause?"

"I'll get a plate for you," Dee said, returning to the cupboard. She assumed the guys would disappear until dinner was ready, but Ted reached out to take the plate when she neared the table.

"We may not be strangers, but this sure is a crowded room," he said quietly.

She saw the twinkle in his eyes before the meaning of his words sank in. "*You* sent the valentine?" she asked incredulously. Stunned, she jumped back and the plate flew out of her hand, shattering.

"Watch it!" Daniel complained.

"Finally, I feel like I'm really back home," her sister said. "She's dropping things again."

"Let me help you clean it up," Ted offered, accepting a broom and dust pan from Deborah.

Dee realized her mouth was hanging open as she squatted to help him. She still couldn't believe the lacy card taped to her mirror had come from Ted. Slowly she mouthed the question racing through her mind. "You?"

"Yes," he answered, keeping his head bent toward the floor. His hair fell over his forehead, so Dee couldn't see his face. "Is it all right?" he asked shyly.

"All right?"

How many times had she wished generous, dependable Ted were her brother instead of Daniel? But thinking of Ted as a brother was one thing, discovering he was her secret admirer was something else. How long had he felt like this about her? And more importantly, how did she feel about him as something more than her brother's friend? The thought wasn't disturbing to her. Just confusing.

He looked up, and the hope in his eyes made her heart beat faster. Again he asked, "Is it OK that the valentine was from me?"

Although confused, Denise was sure of one thing: she didn't want to hurt his feelings. Ted was too nice. "It's fine," she replied, giving him a crooked smile.

He heaved a sigh of relief, and they finished cleaning up the mess.

"Are you done? Is it safe? Can I walk now?" Daniel lifted his foot and placed it down carefully, as if he expected a few of his toes to be severed by shattered china.

Dee looked around the room in surprise. Daniel was being as obnoxious as ever. Deborah was mixing the salad dressing. Her mother was setting mashed potatoes on the table. Her father was rinsing the knife he'd used to cut the meat. *Didn't they notice? Didn't they see what had just happened?*

Ted took the seat opposite Dee at the table. Every time she looked up, he was smiling at her. She didn't dare return his smile, or Daniel would notice and make a scene. But she was dying to talk to him. She had to hook her feet behind the rung on her chair to keep from kicking Ted. What had made him decide to reveal his secret at dinner time? she wondered. He had had a month of opportunities to confess he had left the valentine in her locker. And what was supposed to happen next? A date? She needed to talk to him—alone.

"You must be feeling awfully lonesome without Jeremy," Daniel taunted as they finished the meal.

"Why do you say that?" she asked her brother, finally giving in and grinning at Ted.

"Because you've been making gulleys in your potatoes and watching the butter run out. Looks pretty lovesick to me."

"That's a classic sign," Deborah added.

When Dee saw the sparkle in Ted's eyes, she had to work hard to keep from laughing. Staring at her tunneled potatoes, she said, "Who knows? You could be right."

Daniel didn't answer Dee's remark; Ted did, however. She felt a sneaker nudge her ankle, and she looked up at him. His chin was resting against his hand, and his fingers were curved to shield his mouth from Daniel's view. "Can we talk after dinner?" he asked silently.

She nodded.

For dessert, Dee dished out ice cream and passed around the chocolate-chip cookies her mother had baked that morning. Daniel seemed to inhale his dessert without even chewing. Watching him made Dee so thirsty that she had to go to the sink for a glass of water.

"We rented two video tapes," Daniel announced to the family. "Ted and I are going downstairs to watch them."

"What about the dishes?" Dee asked, hoping to trap Daniel in the kitchen so she could steal a few minutes with Ted.

"You can't fool me," he chanted as he pushed past her. "It's your turn tonight."

Dee was trapped: her brother was right. She sensed someone standing behind her and a curious chill ran down her back.

"I'll try to get away from him," Ted whispered.

"You don't have to," she said over her shoulder. "I'll be down in a few minutes."

The dishes were cleared quickly. Dee rinsed the plates while Deborah set them in the dishwasher. Then she ran a cloth over the counter and hung it on the edge of the sink. "I'm going to watch the movies."

She tramped down the carpeted steps to the family room, where the VCR was hooked up. Daniel and Ted were balancing on the edge of the old couch as an adventurer brushed tarantulas off his assistant.

"Yuck!"

Both guys looked up, and Ted smiled. "Hi!" he said.

Dee saw that she could sit between the guys, or she could squeeze into the spot between Ted and the arm of the couch. She sat on the arm and slid toward Ted. "Scoot over."

"Glad to."

"What are you doing here?" Daniel demanded. "You hate movies with snakes and spiders."

"I know." Dee found it hard to believe he was being so dense. Couldn't he feel the electricity in the air? On the screen, the soldier of fortune squeezed under the descending door just in time to find his assistant dead and bloody. Before she could turn her head, Ted had covered her eyes with his hand.

"I'll tell you when it's safe to look again."

"Thanks." Again his touch sent a shiver down her spine. Dee wondered what was happening to her: she had known Ted for years and never cared if they bumped elbows or touched hands.

"I suppose you're down here because Deborah is having a woman-to-woman talk with Mom," Daniel remarked sarcastically.

"That's part of the reason." Deborah and Mrs. Davidson had started chatting by the time Dee was ready to leave the kitchen, and her sister had made it quite clear that she was not welcome.

"Then why aren't you on the phone with Allison?"

"She's not home from her grandmother's yet."

The second movie was as grim as the first.

Rather than sit with her face covered, Dee tucked her feet beneath her and rested her head on the arm of the couch. She had meant to doze only for a few minutes. Instead, when Ted tickled the soles of her feet, she woke up to find that the movie was already over.

Daniel snapped off the VCR in time to catch the weather report. On the map in front of them, the whole southern half of Minnesota was outlined in a box that said: "Winter storm warning."

"Are you kidding?" Dee asked, wondering how long she'd slept. It looked like a December weather map. Was this some weatherman's idea of a practical joke?

"There are already six inches at the airport," the weatherman reported. "Since eight o'clock, snow has been falling at a rate of an inch per hour. The National Weather Service is now predicting sixteen or more inches by morning. Since the winds picked up in the past hour, *no* travel is advised."

"I guess they're not kidding," Daniel said.

"I'd better go home," Ted said, sounding disappointed. They trudged up the stairs, and Ted got his jacket from the closet.

"Look outside, Ted." Dee's father chuckled. "I don't think you're going anywhere tonight."

Dee pulled back the curtain in the front

window. The whole world was white! The snow was blowing so hard that she could barely see the streetlight two houses away. A drift that started at the window angled all the way up the front door.

"Is the step drifted over?" she asked her father.

"Sure is. And we're not going to shovel it tonight just so Ted can go out there and get lost."

"I'm not arguing," Ted said easily. "I'll just call home so they'll know I'm safe."

Dee was glad he was staying. Every time there was a blizzard, she heard stories about someone who tried to walk a block, only to be found frozen a few steps from their home. But that wasn't the only reason she was happy Ted was staying over. It meant she and Ted would find time to talk.

Ted came back into the living room. "What are we going to do now?"

"Eat and play Monopoly," Daniel answered immediately.

"Monopoly?" Dee asked.

"Yeah. Do you want to play, too?"

"Yeah," she said, angry that her brother had expected to leave her out of the plans. The idea of playing Monopoly wasn't all that exciting to her, but she'd do it if it meant she could be with Ted.

"What do you think?" Daniel asked Ted. "I figured we could have a marathon game. Do you want her to play?"

"Three players will be more fun," he said, winking at Dee.

"OK. We'll get the game ready." He turned to Dee. "You can make popcorn and fix drinks."

"I'll help with the popcorn," Ted volunteered.

"You don't have to do that," Dee's mom said, getting out of her chair. "I'll help her."

Ted followed Daniel to the stairs to the family room. Dee caught his eye before he disappeared from sight, and he shrugged. She knew how he felt. It seemed as if the whole family was conspiring to keep them apart.

The upstairs clock chimed three A.M. Dee covered her mouth to hide a yawn. "Are you ready to declare bankruptcy?" she asked Daniel.

He fanned the few dollars he had left. "No. But if you're tired, I'll mortage Boardwalk and buy you out so you can go to bed."

"No thanks," she replied, handing him the dice. Ted was staring into space, and Dee wondered why the two of them were trying to stay up longer than Daniel. Her brother looked as if he wouldn't fall asleep until after lunch the next day.

"But you've got rehearsal tomorrow," Daniel reminded her. "You should get some sleep."

"I'm not giving up that easily," she said stubbornly. "I won't have practice until the roads are plowed. That gives me plenty of time to break you down. I'm not leaving until I get Boardwalk from you."

"It'll never happen," Daniel declared "So stop dreaming."

"He might be right," Ted said in a tired voice.

Daniel threw a three and moved his token, the shoe, to a Chance square. He drew a card and was told to "Take a ride on the Reading." "Oh, no, not you," he moaned.

Dee giggled and plucked two hundred dollars from his money pile. They had laughed when she'd worked so hard to get all four railroads, but the rents she was collecting assured Dee she'd be in the game for a long time.

Before Ted moved his little dog token around the board, he peered at Dee. "I'll give you five hundred dollars for St. James."

"My answer is still no," she replied, trying to sound tough.

As Daniel took his next turn, Dee realized her legs were stiff. She tried to stretch them out to the side, but her left leg had a mind of its own. The muscles had knotted, and when she tried to move the leg, it jerked toward the board. Houses and hotels jumped into the air and landed all over the game.

"Hey!" Daniel yelled.

"Sorry. It was an accident," she said.

"That's your second accident today. You haven't dropped dishes or kicked things over since you started dating Jeremy. What's wrong with you?"

"Come on. Give me a break." She could feel a blush creeping up her neck. Trying to ignore it, she bent over the board to straighten the buildings, but her arms kept bumping into the hotels she'd already replaced. "Just consider it an earthquake."

"Then what do you call this?" Daniel demanded, picking two houses off her sleeve and tossing them back onto the board.

"An aftershock?" she offered with a grin.

Daniel wrinkled his nose at her joke. "If you didn't know better, Ted, wouldn't you think we had Dee back here with us?"

"I think your sister is fine," he answered gently. Dee felt her blush move up from her neck to her cheeks.

Daniel squinted at his friend. "You must be tired," he said and finished his turn.

"Not too tired to keep playing," Ted said, and took the dice. His dog landed on Community Chest square. He pulled the top card off the stack and read, " 'Go directly to jail. Do not pass Go. Do not collect two hundred dollars.' "

"I'm sorry," Dee said consolingly.

"How come you're never nice to me?" Daniel asked, complaining. "You laugh when I lose money."

"You're my brother," she explained, accepting the dice from Ted. A shiver ran up her arm when their fingers touched. She tossed a five and was instructed to draw a Chance card.

"What's with all the cards?" Daniel joked. "Why don't we start landing on property and paying rents?"

Dee's eyes narrowed as she read her card: "Advance to Boardwalk." Slowly she lifted her token, the thimble, and set it down on Daniel's favorite property, one with two houses on it.

"That will be six hundred dollars, ma'am," he said, rubbing his hands together like a greedy landlord.

"Really?" Before he could grab her hand, she snatched his Boardwalk card and sprinted for the stairs. "You can't collect if you don't have the deed for the property!"

"You snake!" Daniel shouted.

She started up the stairs. "I told you I would get Boardwalk from you. Good night, Daniel—and Ted."

"Come back here, Dee—I mean, Den—"

"Never mind," she called from the top of the stairs. "I think you're right about Dee. She's back."

Chapter Nine

"Over here, Allison," Dee called from a line in a fast-food restaurant in the mall. "I've ordered a soda for each of us."

Allison rushed over and crushed her friend in a bear hug. "It's good to have you back, *Dee*." When she stepped away, Dee adjusted the folds in her baggy red sweater. "And the old clothes are back, too, I see."

"I'll still want to wear my *Denise* clothes sometimes," Dee warned her friend. "But it did feel good to crawl into this top again."

"You look tired," Allison noted, taking two cups from the counter while Dee handed over some change. "Was rehearsal tough?"

"Yeah. Martin works us really hard, but that's not why I'm so tired. You have to hear about Ted."

Allison hustled her friend to a table. "What about Ted?"

"I discovered Tuesday night that *he* gave me the anonymous valentine—"

"No!" Allison's eyes were dancing. "What happened?"

"He got snowed in with us and had to stay the night and most of Wednesday at our house."

"How romantic," Allison said, sighing.

"Not really," Dee told her. "Daniel was with us nearly every second."

"Is he being a jerk?"

"No. He's being stupid." Dee stopped to sip her drink. "When Ted watches me, his eyes shine, and I can't help blushing. But would you believe it? My brother has no idea what's going on."

"Doesn't surprise me. Daniel is about as romantic as a dead turtle. He wouldn't know true love if it slapped him in the face."

"True love?" Dee asked, and laughed. "Don't get carried away. Ted and I are friends."

"Yeah? Well, I wish my friends would send me dreamy valentines. What does Ted say about being friends?"

Dee smiled as she remembered volunteering to help Ted put away the blanket and pillow he'd used for Tuesday night. Cleaning never interested Daniel, so her brother had stayed upstairs in the kitchen to have another piece of French toast.

She and Ted had stared at each other as

they'd folded the blanket. When their hands had touched, he jumped back and she giggled. And after twelve hours of waiting, they finally had a chance to talk, but they'd spent most of their time wondering what to say.

"When we actually managed to dump Daniel," Dee told Allison, "we found out that we didn't know what to say to each other. You know— really talk. He said he likes me, and he invited me to go bowling with him Friday night."

"Sounds like a good start to me," Allison said with satisfaction. The girls got up and dropped their cups into a bin. "Ted is a great guy. You must like him, don't you?"

"Sure, I like him. But the question is, do I *like* him?" Dee asked. They giggled as they strolled out into the mall.

"Yeah, I know," Allison said. "You've always thought of Ted as your adopted brother. You never had to think about him as a real guy until now." Allison stopped in front of the Clothes Hanger to check out the preseason swimsuits. "Are you going on the date?"

"Of course. How else am I going to find out how I feel about Ted?"

"What about Jeremy?"

"Oh, Jeremy," Dee said softly. She'd completely forgotten about him. "You were right about him. He's not my type."

Allison laughed so hard that people turned to look at her. "What took you so long to discover that?"

"What'd you expect? I'm Daniel's sister." Dee knocked on her head. "I didn't see the truth about Jeremy any faster than it's taking him to notice what's happening between Ted and me."

"Let's go over to your house and see the guys," Allison suggested. "Did you drive?"

"No. Ted dropped me off at school for play practice."

Allison raised her eyebrows at the mention of Ted's name. "I've got my mom's car, so let's go."

On the way to Dee's house, Allison continued to ask questions about Ted, but there wasn't much more Dee could tell her friend. There was so much she didn't understand yet about her new relationship with her brother's friend.

When they jumped out of the car, Dee and Allison heard male voices in the Davidson backyard.

"You'll pay for that, Connors!" Daniel yelled playfully.

"Sounds like a snowball fight. Want to join them?" Dee asked Allison, who nodded enthusiastically. Both checked their gear—they were fully equipped with boots, mittens, and scarves.

"Let's go!" they cried in unison and ran around the house.

Daniel saw the girls coming. "We'll have teams," he announced instantly. "Me and Ted against you two."

Dee looked at Ted, expecting him to be disappointed that they couldn't be partners. Instead, she saw that he was grinning devilishly. He couldn't wait to pelt her with snow! she realized. Had he forgotten how good she was at packing and lobbing snowballs?

The snow was wet and heavy—great for making balls that could shoot through the air. Dee and Allison hurried to build up an arsenal. Once the battle started, there'd be little time for packing more weapons.

"Ready?" Daniel yelled to the girls, who were still hunched down, making snowballs. "Go!" Immediately each girl felt a thud against her back.

Dee whipped around with a large snowball in hand. Gleefully she aimed for Ted's shoulder, hoping to make him drop the missile he was readying for her. But before it reached him, he used his pitching arm to wind up and launch a ball in her direction.

Suddenly Dee remembered—the guy was a baseball pitcher! What had she been thinking? She and Allison were going to get creamed.

Ted's snowball buzzed past Dee's head, knocking her hat off as it flew by. She had no time to retrieve it before she retaliated with a slush ball. After that, Daniel tossed a few shots in her direction, and Allison threw a half dozen toward Ted, but Dee and Ted reserved their snowballs for each other.

"Hey, Dee. I thought you'd be taking advantage of this chance to get back at me," Daniel called. He sounded almost jealous that she was ignoring him.

Dee simply could not let his challenge pass. Allison handed her one of their largest snowballs, and she pitched it at her brother's head. She made her shot, but not without cost. While she'd been busy with Daniel, Ted had rushed across their invisible team lines and now he stuffed snow down her neck.

"Ooooo!" she screamed as the icy crystals hit her warm skin. Ted bounced out of arm's reach before she could grab him.

"Good work!" Daniel exclaimed.

"Thank you," Ted answered and took a bow.

"Allison, help me get this out of my shirt!" Dee pleaded, retreating behind an oak tree.

"Now I know he likes you," Allison declared when they were partially hidden by the tree trunk.

"How?" Dee demanded, scooping a handful of snow out of her collar.

"Guys always pick on the girls they like."

"Can we talk about something else? This stuff is starting to melt, and it doesn't make me feel like talking about Ted."

"OK," Allison agreed cheerfully. "Let's talk about play rehearsal. How are you doing as Ado Annie?"

"I love it," Dee replied through clenched teeth as she stretched the bottom of her jacket and sweater, trying to shake out more of the snow.

"How does it feel when the Persian peddler kisses you all the way up your arm?"

"Creepy." Dee shivered from both the memory and her wet clothes. "He's so gross!"

"But you're such a good actress no one'll know you feel that way. Right?"

"Right."

"Then how about your big kiss with the cowboy?"

Dee laughed in embarrassment. "That's not working out so well."

"Why not?" Allison asked, wide-eyed. "Steve is probably the best guy in the play. What's wrong with kissing him?"

"Nothing," Dee replied. "He's supposed to dip me back when he shows me an Oklahoma-hello kiss, but my back won't arch far enough. I'm too stiff."

"That's nothing a little practice won't take care of," Ted said from the other side of the tree.

Suddenly he caught Dee's arm and pulled her around to him. She tripped in the snow and fell against his chest.

"What do you—"

Dee didn't have a chance to finish her question. Ted held her right wrist with one hand, while he slipped his other arm behind her. In a swift move, he bent his body forward at the waist, forcing her backward. She was dipping! she realized, stunned. Apparently her Oklahoma cowboy just didn't know how to do it right.

"That's enough," she said, tapping him on the back. She was getting dizzy.

"No, it's not," he answered, and his lips came down on hers. Ted definitely did not kiss like Jeremy. He was turning her knees into jelly. She stretched her left leg to compensate for her weak knees, and her foot hit some ice. Sure enough, Dee felt herself starting to fall. Desperately she locked her arms around Ted's neck.

"I'm losing my balance," he mumbled just before they crashed to the ground.

Dee's back hit the packed snow, and all the air was knocked out of her. But the second she caught her breath, she started to laugh. She and Ted were certainly not going to forget their first kiss! she thought to herself.

Ted planted a hand in the snow past her left shoulder and pushed himself up to a kneeling position. The startled look on his face soon gave way to an expression of wonder as he gazed at her. Suddenly Dee's mouth went dry. Gently, he reached out a gloved hand to wipe snow off her cheek. "You're so special, Dee. I really like you."

"I like you, too," she said, and her voice caught in her throat. The warmth and love she saw in his eyes had brought her to her senses. Ted was more than an adopted brother to her.

"Why?" he asked.

Why? Did she have to have a reason? She tried to find words to describe her new feelings but was distracted when a pair of black boots crunched down a foot from her head.

"What are you doing with my sister?" Daniel inquired, and the confusion in his voice made Dee smile. "Did you say you *like* her?"

Ted squinted into the noon sun as he looked up at Daniel. "Yes."

"You mean you want to *date* her?"

"Yes."

Daniel made a face that Dee hadn't seen since their mother had tried to make him eat liver. "Are you sure?"

"Lighten up," Ted advised him. "You have to admit I'm an improvement over Jeremy."

Daniel took a few moments to think that over. Finally he nodded. "I suppose."

* * *

At Ted's request, Dee wore jeans and her soft peach-colored sweater on their bowling date. He'd told her he preferred Dee, but Denise had some nice clothes. Dee smiled. Maybe Deborah had been right about guys liking cuddly sweaters, she thought.

"I don't know much about bowling," she told Ted as they leaned down to tie their rented shoes.

"I'll teach you," he volunteered.

"Good luck," she muttered. The last time she had bowled, the manager had congratulated her for breaking the record for gutter balls.

"You can be first," he offered when they reached their lane.

Dee slipped three fingers into the holes of her light blue ball. Then, trying hard to apply Denise's level of concentration to her form, she took five quick steps to the dots on the lane and made her shot.

The ball rolled slowly, but it moved straight ahead. Two pins fell as soon as the ball reached them. A third wavered uncertainly and then tumbled.

"Three! All right!" she cheered, jumping up and down.

"You think three pins is good?" Ted asked from the seat behind the scoring board.

"Sure. I've never hit that many on my first ball before!"

He shook his head and told her to throw her second ball. The moment Dee released the ball this time, she knew it was headed for the gutter. Fascinated, she watched it curve to the right and follow the edge of the lane until it bumped the last pin on that side of the set-up.

"Four points for my first frame." She turned to Ted with a smile—and stopped, dead in her tracks. The look on his face reminded her that in all the time he'd been her brother's best friend they had never bowled together. She bet he was going to be sorry he'd said he would teach her.

"I've never seen a shot quite like that last one," he said carefully as she returned to her seat.

"Neither have I." Dee watched him pick up his ball and approach the lane. He lifted the ball to eye level as if taking measurements. When his arm reached back in a swing, she couldn't help but admire the muscle rippling under his sleeve.

"Darn," he complained when the ball finished its trip down the aisle and left one pin standing. He spent more time aiming the second ball and was rewarded when the final pin clattered to the floor.

"A spare!" she cried.

Ted waited for her to retrieve her ball from the

return slot, then said, "I think I could help you with your form."

"That would be nice," she replied, wondering how close he would have to get to help her.

Ted came up behind her while she held the ball at her side, and she jumped when his hand circled her right wrist. Then something nudged her left foot.

"What're you doing?" she asked, craning her neck to look at his face.

"Trying to get you to move your foot forward. It'll balance your weight better."

She let him push her foot to the proper spot. Then their right arms rose in unison as he prepared to explain about aiming the ball.

Hoots erupted in the next lane. Dee recognized her brother's catcall among the other voices. "I can't look," she said, ducking behind his arm.

"It's Daniel and three other guys from the baseball team," he told her.

"Wonderful," she groaned.

"What good is a girl who can't bowl?" called one of the guys.

"Can't you see how much fun it is to *teach* her?" another kid countered.

"Not when it's my sister," Daniel crooned. "She'll probably drop the ball and break his toe."

"Never mind," he whispered into her ear. She

heard him breathe deeply before saying, "Your hair smells so fresh. I'm glad to see it curly again."

"Thanks." She liked his spicy after-shave, too, and would have said so, but her arm was going to break in another minute. "Could we do something with this ball? It's getting heavy."

He showed her how to line up the ball and helped her practice a few swings. When he thought she had the rhythm down, he stepped back so she could shoot on her own.

Dee was concentrating so hard that she almost bit through her lower lip. Since Ted was really trying to help her, she wanted to do it right—for him.

She took Ted's pose, swung the ball twice, and closed her eyes as she tried to release it. Only it didn't release. Her thumb was stuck. When she shook her hand, the ball flew off.

Clunk. Clunk.

Dee opened her eyes to see the ball jumping from her lane into the next one—her brother's. She cringed, wondering if it would leap over another gutter and interrupt a stranger's game. Ted gasped when the ball suddenly curved and headed straight down Daniel's lane.

Cheers broke out when she knocked down six pins for Daniel's friends. "Good shot, Dee!" her brother cried, laughing.

Dee couldn't help it. She began laughing, too—and the sound echoed. In dismay, she realized her laughter *did* sound like honking birds. Daniel's companions pointed at her in delight. Ted hurried to her side and wrapped his arms around her.

"I'm sorry," she managed to gasp out. She couldn't seem to stop laughing.

"You were just trying too hard," he told her, softly stroking her hair.

"I'm not talking about the bowling ball," she told him, still gasping for air. "I'm sorry for laughing so hard."

He pulled back and stared at her in confusion. "Why?"

"Because I sound like a flock of geese," she said. Inside, Dee wondered if Ted would ever want to take her anywhere in public again.

Ted frowned as he thought about Dee's description of her laugh. "I suppose it's kind of like geese—but happy geese."

Ted was looking more and more like he was the guy for her, she decided, throwing her arms around his neck. She rested her cheek on his chest and sniffed his fresh after-shave. Daniel and his friends hooted again, but Ted didn't seem to care. He just hugged her back.

From then on, Ted continued to throw strikes and spares, and Dee kept trying to improve her aim. Finally she approached the lane for her tenth, and last, frame. Her mouth fell open when eight pins toppled on the first attempt.

"Go for it," Ted told her when the ball returned.

Dee lifted the ball and tried to angle it toward the last two pins. Then, taking a deep breath and holding it, she threw the ball. She didn't breathe again until the two pins wobbled and fell.

"A spare!" she shouted in amazement. She spun around to see a wide smile on Ted's face. Her brother and his friends cheered, and proudly she bowed in their direction.

"You get another ball," Ted reminded her. "It's the last frame."

"That's right," Dee said, setting her jaw with determination. This time, she was going to get a strike. As she took quick steps toward the lane, she imagined all ten pins slamming to the floor. Before she realized it, she'd gone too far forward and her smooth-soled shoes hit the slick surface. Her feet slipped and the ball rolled unceremoniously into the gutter.

Dejected, she shuffled back to Ted. "What a crummy ending."

"But the night's not over yet," he said mysteriously, squeezing her hand.

After he'd taken his last shot, Dee totaled his

score. "One hundred and seventy-five," she announced.

"How about yours?"

"Sixty-five," she muttered.

"Don't worry," he said as he pulled her out of the scorer's chair. "Now we're going to do something you're really good at. And I'm not going to invite your brother."

"What is it?" she asked eagerly, unlacing her shoes.

"We're going to eat hot fudge sundaes."

"What fun!" Dee's spontaneous reaction struck her like a thunderbolt. It was true—she had *fun* with Ted. And that was what made him special. Although Jeremy had taken her to nice places, he'd always made her nervous. Dates with him had not been fun. She was comfortable with Ted, and she knew that was how dates with the right boy were supposed to feel.

Chapter Ten

"I'll leave you two *alone*," Daniel said as he headed upstairs for a Sunday evening snack.

"Sure we're alone," Dee groaned, listening to her mother load the washing machine in the utility room.

"Could I ask you something?" Ted asked Dee. He used the remote control to change television stations while he waited for her answer.

"Sure."

"I've really been curious to know how you changed into Denise."

"Did you like her better?" she asked, stealing the remote back so she could switch to "Solid Gold."

"I only liked her because she was you."

Every time he said something nice like that, her stomach fluttered. "There's not much to tell. I bought some new clothes. I brushed the kinks out of my hair every morning. And I used new cologne and makeup."

"I'm not talking about the outside stuff. You acted different. You didn't trip over your feet anymore or laugh at dumb jokes. How'd you do that?"

She shrugged. "I had to think all the time. Before I opened my mouth, I had to ask myself if what I planned to say was something Denise should say. I couldn't walk into a room until I knew my clothes were on right."

"Was it hard?" he asked, sounding really interested.

"Not at first—I just had to slow down and think. But when I started spending time with Jeremy, I had to be so careful about everything I said and did. I was under a lot of pressure." Her muscles tensed when she remembered the uncomfortable times with Jeremy.

"And how do you feel now?" he asked as he rubbed the tight muscles in the back of her neck.

Dee closed her eyes and tried to relax. Finally Dee did relax, and after a few moments Ted straightened her collar and took his hand away from her neck.

With a sigh, she rested her head on his shoulder. "This vacation has been wonderful. I wish we didn't have to go back to school tomorrow."

"It can't be that bad going back. I'll be there with you."

"I'll have to face Jeremy and tell him about us."

"That could be messy," Ted agreed as he slid his arm behind her on the back of the couch. They both waved at her mother when she started up the stairs.

"Jeremy's been nothing but trouble. I wish I'd never wanted to date him," she grumbled.

"You sound angry. Who are you mad at?"

"Jeremy. Me. Deborah." She shrugged, not really knowing who to blame. "I wasted months chasing Jeremy for all the wrong reasons. You and I could have been having fun together all that time."

"Was the time really wasted?" he asked gently. "Didn't anything good come out of your being Denise?"

She thought about that for a moment. "I guess life was a little easier when I slowed down and took the time to think," she admitted.

"You can still act that way," Ted pointed out. "No one said you have to bounce back to school tomorrow as a clown."

"That's true." Dee frowned. People had liked her as a clown. And people had liked her as Denise. "If I'm not Denise," she said slowly, "and I'm not a clown, who will I be?"

Ted tipped her face up toward his. "You'll be

144

yourself, Dee. You don't have to put on any kind of an act. Think about how you felt as Denise and as your funny self. Starting tomorrow, do the things that feel right."

"It sounds kind of scary."

"I'll be with you," he said softly and pulled her closer to him. She rested against him for a while, feeling safe. Thinking about it, she realized she was actually looking forward to Monday. Letting the real Dee free was going to be a great adventure.

They watched a movie, and at ten o'clock Ted decided he should go home. Dee walked him to the door.

"I'm sorry I wasn't much fun tonight," she told him.

"Don't apologize," he said as he bent to plant a soft kiss on her forehead. "You don't have to be funny for me. I like you just the way you are."

"I'm glad you're here," she told Ted when they met at her locker the next morning.

"You look good," he said, fingering one of the plastic earrings that matched her fuchsia sweater.

"I've wondered what people will say about my old clothes. Do you think they'll know it means Denise is gone?"

"Hi, Dee," called a passing friend from her history class.

"Does that answer your question?" Ted asked, and gave her an understanding smile. "People will probably call you both Dee and Denise if you don't make a fuss."

"I don't mind anymore what they call me." It felt good not to have to worry all the time about an image. Now, if she could just stop worrying about Jeremy. . . .

"Should we look for Jeremy?" Ted asked as if he were reading her mind.

"I don't exactly want to meet him at his locker." In fact, Dee didn't really want to see Jeremy at all until she absolutely had to.

"Well, let's walk in that direction, at least," he suggested and took her hand, swinging it slightly between their bodies.

A few people stopped and stared at Dee. She knew what they were thinking: she'd left for vacation as Jeremy's girl and was returning as Ted's.

"Where's his locker?" Ted asked as they got to the center stairs. "Upstairs or down?"

"It's upstairs around the corner from the drinking fountain." Knowing they would see Jeremy soon, Dee's heart began to pound with dread. Her feet felt as if they were made of lead, and Ted had to tug on her arm to make her keep up with him.

At the top of the stairwell, Dee froze. Jeremy was directly in front of them. It looked as if he'd been starting down to her locker.

"Good morning, Denise," he said politely as his gaze took in her wavy hair, her baggy sweater—and Ted.

"I've got something to tell you," Dee said quickly. "I—"

"I have news, too. Please, let me go first," Jeremy requested. He swallowed hard and stared at her hair and sweater a second time. "What'd you do during vacation?" he asked finally.

"What do you mean, what'd I do? I thought you had something to tell me." Dee knew she was being rude to him, but she didn't care. If she didn't get to spill her news soon, she was going to explode.

"I do, but first tell me about your vacation."

She shrugged and grinned. "I stole Boardwalk." Jeremy's eyes clouded with confusion.

"And she practiced dipping," Ted added.

She jabbed him with her elbow. "And I pitched a few gutter balls. What'd you do, Jeremy?"

"Our shows went well. I especially enjoyed Disney World—"

"Did you visit Epcot Center?" she asked mischievously as she remembered her fantasy about Jeremy getting lost—permanently. Maybe it was mean, but she couldn't resist asking.

"Yeah, we did. I got separated from the group and worried for a while that I'd never get out of there."

She choked back a laugh. "I'm glad you enjoyed the trip. Did you have any other news for me?" Thinking it was time to tell him about her decision, she squeezed Ted's hand for strength and encouragement.

"Actually," Jeremy replied, "something else did happen. Mary Beth Kramer and I finally got together."

"What?!" Dee cried, unable to believe her ears.

Jeremy blushed. "You know Mary Beth, the flute player."

"Sure—"

"I've wanted to date her for a long time."

"I know."

"You do?" He paused for a few seconds, then said, "Well, I'm sorry about how things have turned out." Dee knew he was trying to sound gentle in his own abrupt way, but he was no match for Ted when it came to comforting someone.

"It's OK," she assured him quickly.

He reached out to pat her shoulder. "Thanks for being so brave about it."

"I'm not, really," she admitted, and smiled up at her current boyfriend. "My news for you is that I'm dating Ted now."

"That's—nice. I mean, it's worked out very well. . . ." Jeremy's voice trailed off and he seemed at a loss for words. Dee guessed he thought it was fine for him to dump her, but he clearly had not expected her to find someone else. He'd probably come to school planning to break her heart.

"I guess that's it, then," she said cheerfully. "I wish you and Mary Beth the best."

"Thanks," he muttered, backing away. "The same to you."

As soon as Jeremy was out of sight, she fell against Ted. "I survived!"

He grabbed her left hand and pressed his thumb down on her wrist. "You're right. I can feel your pulse, so you must be alive."

"Very funny," Dee replied. She straightened up and smoothed her sweater.

"You had me worried for a few minutes. Why were you so shocked about Mary Beth? It made me think you still cared about him." He stared down at her and asked shyly, "Do you?"

"Do I still want Jeremy Griffin?" she hooted. "You're crazy to even ask!"

"Then why'd you act stunned when he told you about her?"

She gave him an I-don't-know-why-I-have-to-explain-this look. "Because I couldn't believe how easy he was making this for me. I stayed awake all last night wondering how I was going to tell Jeremy I never wanted to see him again. When he said he was dropping me, I couldn't believe my luck!"

"You're unique," he declared and hooked his arm around her neck, pulling her toward him in a gentle hammerlock. "What other girl would say she was lucky when a guy broke up with her?"

"Any girl who got you in exchange," she whispered. He groaned softly, and she knew her words had touched him. She pulled out of his hug so she could see his face. "Isn't it wonderful to finally be alone?"

He looked around at all the students rushing past them. "Alone?"

"Yes," she answered stubbornly as someone crashed into her back. "My brother is nowhere in sight, and the fear of telling Jeremy is no longer hanging over my head. All I have to think about is you."

"I like that," he said, leading her back to the stairs. "Let's go down and get some juice—my treat—to celebrate your freedom."

Dee smiled. It did feel good to be leaving Jeremy, Denise, and the clown behind.

A crowd had gathered in the hall. Ted and Dee

were about to circle the group on their way to the cafeteria, but curiosity got the better of them and they stopped. Dee raised up on her toes and rested a hand on Ted's shoulder for balance. She saw some of the school athletes standing around a fishbowl. "What is it?" she asked Ted.

Ted turned his head so he could hear what was going on. "Oh," he said finally. "Remember the carnival to raise money for the Ronald McDonald house that's being held on Friday? Well, the lettermen are going to be selling kisses."

Dee grinned. Suddenly she spotted the actor playing the Persian peddler in *Oklahoma!* He was stuffing slips of paper into the fishbowl. For a moment Dee was confused. He had lettered in something? Then she remembered: he had gone to the state golf tournament last spring.

Ted listened a little longer and then told her, "Today they're promoting the carnival by collecting names for a drawing during lunch. Ten lucky girls get free kisses this noon."

Lucky or unlucky? Dee wondered, remembering the way that actor had kissed her arm during play practice. She wasn't going to enter the contest and risk having him slobber on her in the lunchroom.

Someone tugged on her hair from behind. She

turned and saw Allison. "Are you going to put your name in the bowl?" Dee asked her.

"Me? I've already kissed the captain of the football team," she said softly. Although Allison had tried to keep the comment private, people still overheard it and heads cocked all around them to catch the details.

"And?" Dee prompted.

"Once was enough." A few girls snickered, and Ted laughed along with Dee. Allison started to back away from them. "I've got to talk to my counselor about changing a class." She hesitated. "Will I see you at lunch?"

Dee smiled. She knew it was not an idle question. Allison was asking for reassurance. Since Jeremy had taken over her noon hours, she and her friend hadn't had a single lunch together. "Sure, you'll see me at lunch."

"We'll look for you," Ted added, and Dee smiled at his thoughtfulness.

After they waved to Allison, Ted looked down at Dee. "Do you want to put *your* name in the fishbowl?"

Did she? she asked herself. Never mind worrying over the Persian peddler's slobbering—how would she feel about being kissed by one of the school hunks?

If she'd still been dating Jeremy, he would have hustled her through the lobby. And she'd have turned her face away from the action—to avoid temptation. And the old Dee, the clown, would have scribbled her name as fast as was humanly possible and stuffed a handful of entries into the fishbowl. Yes, this was a perfect scene for the clown. But Dee was gone, along with Denise.

"Really, Dee, I don't mind if you want to put your name in for the drawing," Ted said softly, watching her.

"I don't want to," she said, proud that she finally knew her own mind.

"Why not? Are you telling me Allison isn't the only one who's already kissed the football captain?"

"No," she said, firmly turning him to face her. "I'm telling you I would rather have that celebration juice with you."

"Really?" He beamed, eyes sparkling. "You would really rather be with me?"

The pleasure in his voice made her blush. She tugged on his arm until they started moving toward the cafeteria once again. The last time they'd shared a morning juice, he had tried to warn her about Jeremy. Dee shook her head at the memory. She'd been a fool not to listen to him.

Ted dropped some change into the vending machine and carried their glasses to a table.

Before Dee had settled in her chair across from Ted, he was lifting his cup. She touched his wrist before he could take a sip.

"I want to make a toast," she said.

"With orange juice?" he asked and chuckled. The sparkle in his eyes told Dee he thought she was teasing.

She took a deep breath and raised her cup to meet his. "To us—and our new beginning."

The laughter in his eyes faded as his face grew serious. He bumped his cup against Dee's and offered a return toast. "To Dee—I like you just the way you are."